African Twilight
by
Heather Rosser

Contents

Chapter One

The shadowy interior of the hut was a stark contrast to the shimmering heat outside and Jenny paused for a moment in the doorway while her eyes grew accustomed to the half-light.

Huddled on a goat-skin mat was a girl of fifteen or so. Her face lit up when she saw Jenny, then her features contorted with pain and her hands clenched the bead and dove-feather charm she was holding.

There was a muttering from the back of the hut and an old woman shuffled towards the girl proffering a small calabash. She feebly shook her head and looked pleadingly at Jenny who wrinkled her nostrils as she caught a whiff of the acrid-smelling concoction.

"How long have you been in labour?"

Jenny felt the words ring out harshly and she winced at the sound of her carefully-enunciated question. It was cool in the hut but she felt her cotton dress sticking to her and her brown shoulder-length hair clinging to the nape of her neck.

"Yesterday," the girl whispered.

What am I going to do? thought Jenny desperately. I'm not a nurse. I'll have to get her to the hospital.

She glanced at the old woman who was dipping her finger in the potion and rubbing it on to the girl's lips.

If only I knew more about this country. And what am I doing interfering with their customs anyway? Jenny felt her head pound as her thoughts raced.

She drew a deep breath and squatted beside her young friend.

"Patience," she said taking the thin black hand in hers, "shall I get the doctor?"

The girl started to nod then glanced anxiously at her grandmother whose wizened form had once again merged with the shadows at the back of the hut.

She let out a torrent of abuse and sprang towards Jenny shaking her finger in admonishment.

"It's alright," Jenny spoke in halting Chakari. She stood up and walked to the door. "I'll be back soon," she said to Patience in English.

She screwed up her eyes as she went back into the sunlight. A small band of children were kicking an ancient tennis ball around the compound. She smiled as she caught a glimpse of a small brown and even smaller blonde head amongst the black curly ones.

I can't leave them here while I go for Richard. Jenny stood uncertainly, wondering what to do.

It was only two weeks since she had first met the Ntoo family. Her American friend Sue, a teacher at the secondary school, had introduced her. Patience had been one of her students until she became pregnant. Jenny had been excited about meeting a Charkian family so soon after her arrival and she had visited them several times since.

She smiled with relief as a woman about the same age as herself entered the compound. She was wearing a faded cotton wrapper and blouse and a pink nylon scarf around her head.

The two women greeted each other in Chakari.

"I think Patience needs help," said Jenny.

"Yes," said Mrs Ntoo searching for the right words in English, "I have sent for the witchdoctor."

Jenny looked askance. She had been in Chark long enough to know that, while the witchdoctor was able to cure a variety of ailments as well or even better than the western medicine dispensed at the hospital, there was little he could do for complications in childbirth.

"I think your daughter should go to hospital." Jenny felt her voice tremble in her anxiety.

"It is not our custom," replied the woman calmly.

"That's cassava. We use the roots for cooking," said Amos.

"High in carbohydrate but contains no protein," murmured Richard.

Jenny glanced round sharply and was relieved to see that Amos and his cousin had walked on and were showing James a vegetable garden surrounded by a hedge made of cut branches. The three men walked slowly among the rows of tomatoes, onions and peppers, often stopping to examine a plant in detail.

"That looks like a good crop," said Richard when they reached them.

"Yes, things are growing well this year. At the moment we are only growing enough for our personal use, plus a small surplus that Ezekiel's wife sells in the village. We hope to expand it and sell the vegetables in Bambo, but transportation will be a problem."

"Do you have any trouble from predators?" asked Jenny.

"We do have a problem with porcupines but on the whole we are lucky, there is very little game in this area."

There was a sudden commotion and several reddish-brown cows trampled down the bank and into the river.

"Apart from cows," said Richard.

"Cows? Oh yes of course." Amos laughed politely.

There was a splatter in the water.

"It's doing a poo! "said Darren in amazement.

"Cow poo!" chuckled David pointing delightedly.

Further up-stream a girl from the compound appeared carrying a bucket. She went to the water's edge, stooped down and filled it. Then she lifted the bucket carefully on to her head, turned around and walked back along the path to the compound.

Jenny and Richard looked at each other and grimaced.

"How many cattle do you have?" asked James.

Amos turned to Ezekiel and spoke in Chakari.

"About seventy-five," he replied. "We will go and look at the sorghum and then on to the kraal."

Amos led the way along the river bank and then they turned and found themselves in front of a swaying forest of sorghum. The stalks were thick and rose above their heads. Amos put his hand up and pulled one of the stalks down so that they could examine the head.

"This one is almost ready," he said looking at the rust-coloured seeds making up the sorghum head that was nearly as large as his hand.

They walked along the rows stopping every now and then to examine the plants. Underfoot were watermelons and they had to tread carefully.

"I think they're going to walk up and down every row," whispered Jenny to
Richard.

"Okay, we'll meet them at the edge of the field."

"Gosh, it's hot," Jenny shaded her eyes as they emerged from the shade of the sorghum.

"I wonder how much longer we're going to be," said Richard looking at his watch.

"I shouldn't think they'll be long. There can't be too much to say about one field of sorghum even if James is an agricultural expert."

"No I don't mean in the field. I wonder when we'll go home."

"Home? But we're here for the day aren't we? What do you want to go home for?"

"I'm a bit worried about Mr. Salla's compound fracture. I set his leg on Friday and it needs careful checking, we don't want gangrene to set in."

Jenny looked incredulous. "But Dr. Patel's there."

"He's only on call on Sunday and Sister Everett is off this week-end. In any case Dr. Patel doesn't specialize in orthopaedics."

Jenny felt herself go tense with anger. She drew in a breath, started to speak, then was checked by a voice inside her.

"Don't spoil the day," it seemed to say. She relaxed and smiled at Ezekiel's children who had joined them and stood giggling shyly. A girl of about eight took Darren's hand. "Come with me," she said and they walked along the path together. The others followed and they skirted the field. They had just reached the far side when they met Amos, Ezekiel and James deep in conversation.

"Ah, this man knows a lot," said Amos expansively clapping James on the shoulder. He looked at Jenny. "How is the sun Mrs. North? If you are too hot we will go back now."

"No, we're just fine," she replied not looking at Richard. They left the sorghum field and walked along a sandy path. The sun was high in the sky and David's hand felt damp in Jenny's as they trudged along behind the others. The tinkling of cow bells could be heard around them and the resonant lowing told them that they were nearing the kraal.

They paused to look at the two cows with their calves standing patiently behind the thorn hedge of the kraal. Amos told them that the rest of the cattle were foraging throughout the farm. then he took out his handkerchief and mopped the sweat off his brow.

"So now you have seen most of the farm, "he said turning to Jenny and Richard. "How do you like it? Or is it too hot for you?"

"It's very interesting but it is getting hot," said Richard putting David on his shoulders.

"We are not far from the compound," Amos started to lead the way past the kraal.

Five minutes later they saw the thatched roofs of the huts. The children ran ahead and soon Jenny and Richard were seated in the folding chairs again. The tea things had been cleared away but the table remained.

Amos went into the hut and brought out a skin mat which he put down near Jenny.

"Darren and David, you can sit here," he said.

They made themselves comfortable and then the girl appeared again with a tray. This time there were six plates and spoons, two enamel dishes and a bowl of water. She held the bowl in front of Amos and poured a little water onto his hands. He washed them letting the water drip on to the ground. When they had all washed their hands in this way, Amos gestured to Jenny to serve the food. She lifted the lids off the dishes. One was piled high with hard sorghum porridge, the other contained a chicken cooked with a variety of fragrant spices. Jenny hesitated and looked at the six plates and then at the children standing watching.

"What about the others?" she asked.

"They will have their meal this evening," said Amos.

Jenny obediently served portions to the boys and then to Amos, James, Richard and herself. She absently watched the chickens scratch about as she chewed the tough meat. She thought of the morning's chase to catch the little black hen then suddenly felt her stomach heave as she realised that it was the black hen they were eating now.

She looked at Richard but he appeared to have no qualms about what he was eating. Jenny relaxed. She listened with half an ear while Richard asked Amos about his cattle and Amos talked about his plans to expand the farm when he retired.

I hope we can come here again, thought Jenny as she put her empty plate down. It's good for us all to get away from the hospital compound.

She yawned. A fly buzzed around her head but she did not see it because her eyes were closed and she was almost asleep.

Chapter Four

It was a dark, starless night and Jenny sat on the verandah flicking idly through the pages of Cosmopolitan. She had bought the magazine a couple of weeks earlier in Nomads. It had been the first holiday Richard had taken in the sixteen months that he had worked in Bambo.
And now it was over.

Jenny sighed and stared ahead of her. The air was hot and sticky and she felt listless. There was a persistent hum of mosquitoes and every now and again she hit out with the magazine as an insect landed on her. During the last six months she had felt increasingly dissatisfied with her life in Bambo but she had tried to remain cheerful and hoped that the holiday would restore her spirits. She was dismayed to find on her return that, instead of recovering her old enthusiasm for life, she was perpetually tired. Richard was spending even more time working, the boys were bigger and more demanding and she, herself, felt worthless.

"January, February, March........" she muttered counting the months to the end of Richard's contract on her fingers. Eight-and-a-half months. Unless he decided to extend it. Would he? Could she bear it if he did? Would it be fair of her to stand in his way knowing that he enjoyed his work so much? The questions made her head spin. If only she had someone to talk to. When she had so enthusiastically agreed to Richard's proposal that they go to Chark she had no idea that she would suffer such loneliness. She scowled, angry with herself. Self-pity was something that she had rarely indulged in even after the death of her parents. It's just a question of keeping busy she told herself.

She picked up the magazine and went into the house. The heat was stifling and she nearly went out again but the thought of the mosquitoes decided her against it. She almost wished that the boys would wake up, at least they would be company while Richard was working.

This is ridiculous she thought, Richard was often working in the evenings in England. But it was different back home, there was always plenty to do. And if she got fed up she could ring Pam for a chat, or Pam would ring her or drop round unexpectedly. If she could only pick up the phone now and talk to her friend she knew she would feel better.

Well, I'd better do the next best thing and write a letter, she told herself in a determined attempt to pull herself together.

She got her type-writer and settled down to write.

Bambo. Jan. 12th.
Dear Pam,
It was so nice to have your card from the Bahamas waiting for us when we got back from our trip to Mombasa. I look forward to hearing more about it- and your new boyfriend - when you have time to write a letter.
We had an enjoyable holiday although it didn't quite live up to my expectations. I think I had been looking forward to it too much.
We had originally planned to drive there and I got very excited about that, planning the route and what we would need to take and how much we could pack in the Beetle. Richard had only taken a couple of days leave since we arrived and so, by going over Christmas, we were going to have three weeks away. He had been working much too hard and really needed a long break from the hospital. Then at the last minute he said that he could only be away two weeks. He tried to tell me that this was a Ministry decision but frankly I

didn't believe him. Dr. Patel has just gone on leave for three months leaving the hospital with only one doctor so surely they could have managed with one doctor for three weeks.

So, as our holiday was cut down to two weeks, Richard decided it would be better to fly. I said that I considered the drive would be part of the holiday but he didn't agree and, as it was him who really needed the holiday, I gave in. In the end it took two days to get there by plane because we had to drive to Munari and then hang around at each airport waiting for connecting flights as the most suitable ones were full because we had made our bookings so late.

We rented a holiday flat, beautifully situated right on the ocean. We were able to run down and have a swim before breakfast. The sea was lovely and warm and the boys really enjoyed it. Darren learnt to swim, it's such a pity he can't keep it up now we're home again. We had several trips out to the coral reef. Richard and I hired snorkels and it was fascinating watching the fish swimming amongst the coral.

There was a steward who cleaned the flat so that wasn't a problem and there was a cheap restaurant nearby where we sometimes ate. We had picnics most of the time though. There was plenty of fresh fruit to buy especially coconuts which we all enjoyed. In fact the "beach" part of the holiday was super, Richard relaxed and the boys didn't irritate me as much as usual because they were so occupied in and around the water. They did need constant watching though.

However I didn't feel I had gone all that way
to sit on the beach all day. I wanted to
explore the city and go out to dinner or a
disco as well. I also wanted to do some
shopping especially clothes for the boys as
they had grown out of most of their things.
It wasn't easy to prise Richard off the beach
but the boys were eager to get the bus into
town and so we went. When we got off in the
city centre the boys went wild with all the
traffic. They started running up and down the
street shouting (trying to make more noise
than the traffic I suppose). Darren had
forgotten all the road sense he once had and
I was terrified in case he ran under a car.
David was so excited when he saw some traffic
lights, he kept shouting and pointing at them
and I saw a lady smile at him and I felt as
if we were real "up-country" family.
I thought things would be better once we got
inside a shop but if anything it was worse.
They wanted to touch everything like they do
in the market in Bambo. Everybody was in a
hurry and it was all quite bewildering. I
kept telling myself that only sixteen months
previously I had taken the boys shopping in
London without a qualm. But since then I
seemed to have lost my urban survival
techniques. Richard was no help at all and
just looked around in a glazed fashion
mumbling "Let's get out of here". At one
point we were separated and I caught sight of
him from a distance and he seemed much
smaller, almost insignificant. I suppose I'm
used to seeing him either at home or walking
briskly in his spotless white coat. Suddenly
I saw him as "just a man" and I felt

frightened as if something had dropped and shattered.

I had a similar feeling the following evening when we went for dinner at a hotel just along the beach from our flat. We hadn't been keen to use the baby sitting service provided by the flats but we did want an evening out together so we hired a very nice lady to look after the boys. It was a romantic walk along the beach with the waves lapping against the shore and a shaft of moonlight streaming across the coral reef. The hotel was full of holiday-makers from Europe and we enjoyed watching the people while we ate. Afterwards we sat outside on the patio where the band was playing. It was quite crowded and we were joined by two other couples, not holiday-makers from Europe but expatriates working in Nairobi.

The women were well-dressed and, despite the fact that I was wearing clothes I had bought in London just before we came here, I felt out of place. Maybe I was being over-sensitive but I felt that they looked at my dusty sandals disapprovingly. I wanted to say that I used to wear elegant shoes like theirs when I went to parties but when you walk mainly on dirt roads they aren't practical. I found I didn't have much to say to them - our lives were worlds apart, I didn't think they would be interested in hearing about our walks through Bambo. I have always been satisfied with the fact that we can buy basic commodities at the market but they seemed horrified that we have to rely mainly on local produce. It seems that

most of their purchases are flown in from
Europe.
The men were interested in discussing African
politics and, although I disagreed with their
viewpoint, they seemed quite knowledgeable.
Not like Richard. It was only then that I
realised how little interest he takes in
anything except the hospital. He doesn't
know the names of any of the Charkian
ministers except the Minister of Health. I
sometimes take the boys to Larry and Sue at
the secondary school when Richard is working
and their house is often full of teachers
discussing politics. When I mentioned it to
him once he said that it was alright for
teachers to sit around talking but he had
work to do. He would probably enjoy the
company of other doctors but it requires too
much effort to tune into teachers. He still
spends a lot of his spare time reading
medical journals so that he can cope with the
great variety of cases he has to treat. We
had agreed that while we were on holiday we
would try not to mention that Richard is a
doctor but without that to talk about,
conversation is limited. We mentioned the
boys but when our companions realised that
Darren was nearly six and not even going to
nursery school they were scandalized.
In fact we are becoming worried about
Darren's education and I have started giving
him some lessons. I don't find it easy and
he would rather be out playing. I'm afraid
the lessons often end in tears. I had a
letter from a friend at home whose little boy
used to go to the same playschool as Darren.
He has now been at school nearly a year and

was even in a school concert. I wonder whether it matters that Darren is missing out on the benefits of formal education or whether what he is absorbing by playing with his Charkian friends compensates. In her letter my friend said that she has just started a part-time job. She said that I must be leading an interesting life but in fact I'm beginning to feel rather hemmed in. Of course there is no opportunity for me to work in Bambo. I sometimes used to think that life here was like living in a back-water but now I don't even feel it's like that - back-waters are usually close to the main stream but in Bambo I feel increasingly isolated from everything.

A few months ago I suggested to Richard that I did some voluntary work in the hospital. He thought it was a good idea because they are understaffed and many of the nurses consider themselves too important to really talk to the patients or help them with the little things. Richard gets very upset about the fact that there is no physiotherapist or even any concept of it and he thought I could work with the orthopaedic patients. I also thought I could spend some time in the children's ward. Of course there are no toys but Larry asked the woodwork teacher at the secondary school to give him the off-cuts and he planed them down and brought us a nice box of building blocks. I became quite enthusiastic and planned to leave the boys with Isaac for a couple of hours two afternoons a week. The day before I planned to start Richard said that, out of courtesy, I should mention the matter to matron. So I

went to see her in her office. She was busy
writing when the nurse showed me in and she
didn't look up for a while. When she did she
didn't offer me a chair and she made me feel
like a schoolgirl. She just sat looking at
me while I tried to explain what I was going
to do then she suddenly interrupted and asked
what my qualifications were. I was so taken
aback I couldn't think of anything to say.
Then she said that Chark was a developing
country and they couldn't afford such
luxuries. I told her that I was going to do
the work for nothing, that I didn't even
consider it work. She said she thanked me
for my interest but it wasn't hospital policy
to employ unqualified people. Richard tried
again later and told her how the N.H.S.
relies on voluntary workers but she wouldn't
change her mind. Miss Everett told us
afterwards that hospitals in Africa are very
wary about expatriates and in any case the
concept of voluntary work is alien. She took
the bricks to the children's ward but found
it difficult to persuade the nurses to use
them constructively with the children.
Matron's niece passed her maths and she is
now at college in Munari. It's only since
she's gone that I realised how much I enjoyed
our sessions together. Darren is missing
Joshua now that he has started school though
they still play together most afternoons.
We are still waiting for another doctor. It
would be so nice if someone with a young
family moved into the empty house.
We were just beginning to get to know James,
the agricultural officer, when he was

transferred to Mutape. But maybe I told you
that in a previous letter.
I seem to have gone on at length but it's
been a relief writing it all down. It will
be so good to see you and exchange all our
news. I wish you were coming sooner but June
will be a good time because the rains will
have stopped then. I suggested to Richard
that he takes some leave and we can go up to
Mutape and maybe head west into the
mountains.
Let me know as soon as you can what date you
are coming.
By the time you come I should know what our
plans are. Richard's contract is due to
finish in September but he is talking about
extending. He's certainly needed but maybe
that will change if a new doctor is posted
here. I hope it will be soon and then
perhaps Richard will stop working so hard.
Looking forward to hearing from you.

Love,
Jenny.

Chapter Five

"Quiet boys!" Jenny snapped as she wrenched the steering wheel of the Beetle to avoid a rock. The road became steeper as it neared the rest house and she flung the car into second gear. The engine spluttered and for a moment Jenny thought it was going to stop.

"Dam those plugs," she muttered.

She knew she should have the car serviced but she was afraid of losing the use of it even if it was for only a day, though it would probably be a week at the garage in Bambo.

Over the last few months she had increasingly regarded the car as a life-line. It was her way of getting out of the hospital compound. In point of fact she did not use it that often, there were not many places to go and she still enjoyed walking into town although she was becoming increasingly irritated at the way the boys walked, either at a snail's pace as they discussed every stone they picked up or dashing ahead so quickly that she was panting by the time she reached them.

She glanced in the rear view mirror which she had adjusted so that she could see her children. Darren had shot up in the last year and seemed all arms and legs. His brown hair fell over his eyes. Richard had reproached her only that morning for not cutting it, but cutting Darren's hair was such a battle that Jenny usually put it off until he could hardly see through it.

She caught sight of David's blue eyes looking at her anxiously. He had changed from a baby into a little boy but he was still a cuddly child and enjoyed curling up on Jenny's knee.

Jenny sighed and made an effort to relax. It was not the boys' fault that her evening out with Richard was ruined. It was her birthday and they had planned to go to the rest house for a meal while Sister Everett looked after the boys.

Jenny had been looking forward to it because they had not been anywhere on their own together since their holiday at Christmas and it was now the first of May. Richard and Sister Everett had been on duty since eight o'clock and were due to finish at five but at four o'clock news came that a bus   had overturned. Amos cancelled everyone's off-duty and sent messages recalling nurses who were already off to come back and care for the injured.

Richard had suggested apologetically that Jenny take the boys to the rest house. She had not been keen on taking them out and being on edge watching that they behaved themselves, but it seemed preferable to staying at home. She hoped that there would not be many people there, she did not feel she could cope with a crowd especially if they were strangers.

As she drove through the gateway Jenny noticed two Charkian men in earnest conversation at one of the tables. There was no-one else in sight.

"Leave that door alone!" she screamed as Darren leant over the passenger seat to open the door before she had parked the car. She was upset to feel tears stinging her eyes. She had been so certain that she would see Sue's friendly face that she felt she could not bear to get out of the car.

"Sit down will you," she yelled at Darren who had climbed onto the front seat in his impatience to get out. "No, in the back, we're going home," her voice trembled as she tried to ignore the bewildered faces of her sons.

She swung the car round revving fiercely. The noise made the men look up. The larger of the two glared at her with such a look of dislike that Jenny was pleased she had decided not to stay. The slimmer man however got up and walked towards them. Jenny's heart started to thump as she waited to hear what he had to say. She put on the hand-brake but kept the engine running and drew in her breath with irritation as Darren scrambled out of the car and ran towards the man calling "hello".

"Hello Darren," he replied smiling down at the eager child. Jenny started and leant out of the window looking at the man properly for the first time.

"Why it's, it's James!" she stammered switching off the engine and getting slowly out of the car.

"I'm sorry I didn't recognize you, "she said looking at him searchingly.

His clothes were still immaculate but he had lost weight and he looked older. The arrogant tilt to the head which she had noticed when they first met seemed more pronounced, while in contrast the cigarette between his fingers gave him a slightly degenerate look.

"Oh, we blacks all look alike," he said lightly as he blew smoke from his nostrils.

Jenny blushed with embarrassment and anger at his remark.

"It's just that I thought you were in Mutape," she said. "We haven't seen you for some time."

James looked around. "Where's your husband?" he asked. "He's working. Come Darren, we're going home now."

"But surely you are going to have a drink." He looked at her intently. "You look tired, a drink will do you good." Jenny followed him mutely to the table. It was true, the disappointment, anger and frustration she had felt that afternoon had made her feel tired. She would just have a quick drink then take the boys home and have an early night.

As they approached the table the large man stared insolently at Jenny then looked at James with an enquiring grin.

James frowned and pulled out a chair for her. "I would like you to meet Jenny North from Britain. Her husband is a doctor at the hospital. And these are her two sons. Jenny this is Leintu, a cousin of mine."

"How do you do," said Jenny formally putting out her hand.

"Pleased to meet you," grunted Leintu unconvincingly as he shook her hand. His shorts and floral open-necked shirt seemed to emphasise the bulk of his large frame.

"What would you like to drink?" James beckoned the steward who was hovering in the door of the rest house.

"Beer please," said Jenny looking at the empty bottles on the table.

"Three beers and two cokes," said James to the elderly steward.

"Have you been back in Bambo long?" asked Jenny.

"Only a few days, but long enough to see that nothing has been done in my absence." James's voice had a tone that Jenny could not remember hearing before. It had a bitter note and he weighed his words carefully as if he were very weary.

"I expect you were sorry to leave Mutape." Jenny sensed that this was the wrong thing to say but she did not want to sit in silence. She was aware of Leintu sitting back in his chair cracking his knuckles as he looked at her through narrowed eyes.

"They replaced me with a man from Munari." James stared into the distance, his face grim.

She was relieved when the steward reappeared with the drinks. James put his hand in his pocket but Leintu was already ostentatiously peeling off a couple of notes from a wad in his hand.

"My round," he growled throwing the notes on the tray.

"Thank you," said Jenny uncertainly.

"I want to open mine," said Darren picking up the can and shaking it. Before she could stop him he had pulled the cap off and coke spurted out all over the steward. The man stepped back blinking in surprise as he wiped his sleeve across his face. He looked down in bewilderment at the brown liquid seeping into his jacket.

"Darren!" exclaimed Jenny, then stopped. Leintu was roaring with laughter. He put another note on the tray and told the man to bring another coke.

"I'm sorry," said Jenny to the departing steward.

"Oh don't worry about him," drawled Leintu wiping the tears from his eyes with a scarlet handkerchief. "That was a good aim boy but you better drink the next one eh."

Darren looked confused. He had not pointed the can at the steward on purpose and he knew his mother was angry with him. He looked enquiring at James.

"How old are you Darren?" asked James thoughtfully.

"I'm six. I shall go to school soon," said Darren proudly.

"And where will you go to school?"

"I'm going with Joshua to the school near the hospital."

James raised his eyebrows questioningly at Jenny.

Jenny hesitated. She was aware of Leintu appraising her in an indolent way and James's comment when they had met was still ringing in her ears.

"We haven't decided yet," she said. "Richard's contract finishes in four months and we don't know whether to extend it or not. If we stay I think we'll let Darren go to school here. I'm giving him a few lessons at home but he needs a bit of school discipline I think.

Jenny sighed and thought of the visit she had made to the school. There were sixty children in the first class. They had been sitting on hard wooden forms chanting when she had looked in. Apart from a portrait of the President, the walls were bare although the teacher had apologised for this and explained how difficult it was to get anything to stick on the rough plaster. The class-room had no ceiling and the tin roof made it very hot.

James nodded abstractedly. "Yes, this business of making decisions is not easy. He won't come to any harm at school anyway."

Jenny looked grateful. "No, I'm sure he won't."

The steward arrived with another coke, this time already in a glass.

Leintu grinned as he took his change. "The old man isn't taking any chances this time," he said handing Darren the glass.

"Have you been to Amos's farm again?" asked James.

"We had planned to go there before Christmas but David was sick so we couldn't go. And since Christmas Richard hasn't had much time off with Dr. Patel being on leave but now that he's back and Dr. Fatti has arrived things should be much better."

"Daddy's busy," announced David solemnly as he drained his glass leaving a moustache around his mouth.

James gave a half smile but did not answer as he drummed his fingers on his cigarette packet.

Jenny poured the rest of her beer into her glass but did not want to drink it too quickly. She strained her ears in case she could hear the sound of Larry and Sue's motor bike. As she watched the sun beginning to sink she was aware of Leintu sitting back looking her up and down.

"Have you never seen a white woman before?" Jenny wanted to cry but she said nothing as she unconsciously crossed her legs.

Darren and David had got down from the table and were examining the corn cobs ripening on the small patch of maize.

"Don't pick them," called Jenny. She turned to James. "I took your advice and planted maize by the tap in the back garden. We've had a good crop this year."

"That is good. And how are the water melons? Did you plant some under the maize?"

"Yes, and pumpkins too. In fact they've nearly taken over the garden. They have travelled a long way from the maize bed. We've eaten some but there's a lot more still ripening."

"You are fortunate that you can water your garden. The rains haven't been very good this year."

"There won't be any more rain this season," predicted Leintu.

James looked angry. "You know you cannot be certain. We often have rain in May when the whole season has been good. We will probably get a few showers but the real rains have finished."

Jenny looked from one to the other feeling the tension between the two men. James's face looked darker and Jenny thought his hand trembled as he lifted his glass to his mouth.

She wondered what had happened to him since he had been away. He had been so pleased when he heard that his application for a transfer to Mutape had been approved. He must be disappointed to be back in Bambo again and yet Jenny felt it was more than disappointment that had caused the change in him.

She was just about to ask him if he had been ill when a battered white Peugeot 404 turned into the gateway. It parked under the bougainvillea next to Jenny's Beetle and Larry and Sue got out of the back seats. Jenny recognised the driver as Hans, a Dutchman who had recently come to the secondary school. The fourth passenger was a Charkian whom she had not met before.

"Hi there!" called Sue as they walked towards the table. "How's things Jenny? James, It's good to see you again. How are you doing? Have you met Hans from the Netherlands and Nelson from Munari? They're both teachers at school."

Everyone shook hands and brought more chairs to the table. Larry called the steward and ordered a round of drinks.

"Richard working?" enquired Larry.

Jenny grimaced. "As usual," she laughed. "We'd planned to come out to dinner tonight but a bus overturned so Richard had to stay to deal with the injured."

"That's terrible," said Sue. "Where did it happen? Were many people hurt?"

Jenny looked disconcerted. She had not thought of the accident in terms of people.

"Richard didn't have time to tell me any details. He just said we'd have to cancel our evening out and suggested I came out for a drink with the boys."

Sue looked sympathetic. "That's a shame. Were you celebrating anything special?"

"Only my birthday," Jenny gave a rueful laugh.

"Your birthday. That calls for a bottle of champagne!" said Larry. He called the steward.

"No champagne sir," said the steward. "We got white wine, whisky, brandy, beer, but champagne finished."

"Don't worry," said Jenny. "Beer's fine." she looked at the gold and crimson streaks glowing where the sun had just set. "We must be going soon anyway."

"Just relax, the kids are fine," said Sue nodding at the boys who were happily filling empty bottles with sand.

"Happy birthday Jenny," said James raising his glass.

"Thank you," said Jenny meeting his eyes for a moment and then looking away.

She turned to Nelson. He was small, neatly dressed and looked very young. "We haven't met before. Have you been at the school long?"

"No, just a month. I was teaching in Munari before but they transferred me because there wasn't an economics teacher in Bambo."

Leintu snorted. "Economics! What do you want to teach economics for?"

Nelson replied defensively, "It is very important for a developing nation to have a grasp of economic principles."

"Who in the nation should have an understanding of these principles?"

"Well. everybody."

Leintu glared at him.

Nelson appeared to shrink in the face of this cross-questioning. "Well, the nation's leaders are the ones to formulate economic policy."

"So they, more than anyone, should have a fundamental grasp of economics?"

"Well, yes - of course."

"Of course, he says. And do they? Is it good economic policy to import foodstuffs when with a little encouragement our own farmers can produce enough to feed everybody? Of course the foreign powers who we are increasingly dependent on would rather spend millions of dollars on updating our airports to fly in their expensive cargo than a few thousand in improving rural roads so that small farmers can sell their products in the nearest market town."

Leintu settled back in his chair and glowered, at the four white faces.

Nelson looked relieved and took a long draught of beer.

Leintu turned to him again. "The politicians in Munari have forgotten about the rural areas. In my father's village the oranges rot on the trees because the people are not able to transport them even as far as Mutape. And what do you see in the supermarket in Munari? Imported oranges and marmalade. Marmalade!" he spat the word out.

Larry looked puzzled. "But if there is so much surplus fruit why doesn't the government open a canning factory to deal with it?"

James spoke quietly, "Most of the citrus growing areas are in the north where there is more rain. And the black cotton soil makes it expensive to build roads. And in any case," here he paused to give emphasis to his words, "the north is not a high priority area."

"But what about the oil?" asked Hans speaking for the first time.

James weighed his words carefully. "The revenue from the oil should help but it does not appear to be used for the benefit of the people living in the area."

"Mutape seemed to be pretty well developed when we were there," observed Sue.

"Mutape has its prestige projects. The Vandu Hotel is probably as good as many you will find in America. And the town has electricity and a good water supply. But you only have to travel a few kilometres out of the town to find villages without even a standpipe. Some people have to walk two or three kilometres for water."

James stopped speaking as the steward came to collect the glasses. He ordered another round of drinks.

Nelson looked back at the group, opened his mouth as if to speak and then shut it again.

Leintu leant back in his chair surveying the scene with apparent detachment. He raised his hand. "The economics teacher has something to say," he drawled.

Nelson gulped his beer and answered angrily. "The oil revenue is just beginning to come in, it will be a while before the benefits are felt. And anyway it provides jobs for the Ntisi."

"Jobs for the Ntisi does it?" Leintu's voice was icy. "If you study the employment structure of the industry you will find that practically all the managerial and technical posts are held by expatriates. There are of course a few," here he paused to give added weight to his words, "Charkians who have been posted from Munari to act as window dressing."

"But surely there must be lots of jobs created by the expansion of Mutape," said Hans.

James spoke again. "The building industry certainly provides reasonably well-paid short-term employment. All the young people and many of the older men are leaving the villages in search of work in the city. But what will happen when the building programme is complete? They won't want to return to subsistence farming."

Sue looked at him earnestly. "But what can be done about it?"

"If the oil revenue was used to improve farming and its associated industries that would be money well spent." He looked at Larry. "They could indeed set up a canning factory in the centre growing area. They could...... Jenny, are you alright?"

Jenny had suddenly got up and was looking anxiously about her.

"It's the boys, I can't see them. They were playing there," she said distractedly pointing towards the vegetable patch. It was difficult to see because it was dark now and the light from the rest house was throwing out dark shadows.

"Well they can't have gone far," said Larry getting up.

"Perhaps they went inside," suggested James walking towards the building.

But Jenny was already running behind the vegetable patch and towards the thatched huts that provided sleeping accommodation for guests. Her heart was pounding as she tried to fight away images of scorpions and black mambas. The first hut that she came to was unlit. She stumbled around it stubbing her toe on a stone as she went.

"What are you doing?" she said to herself. "They won't be here in the dark."

"But maybe they are lying unable to move," her other voice answered.

"Don't be silly, you'd have heard them cry if anything was the matter."

"Maybe they're out of earshot, maybe they went out of the gate." The other voice was insistent and Jenny's heart beat louder and her breath came in short gasps as she ran towards the next hut.

Light was streaming from the window and, as she came nearer, the door opened and a man stood in the doorway. "Are you alright?" he asked. His voice was warm and his face full of concern as he looked down at Jenny.

"I've lost, I'm looking for, my little boys," she stammered looking up at his tanned face. The light shining from behind enabled Jenny to take in his appearance easily. He was tall and broad-shouldered with blonde hair and hazel-coloured eyes. As Jenny looked at him she was momentarily glad that she was standing in the shadow. She did not feel she wanted this man to see her distraught face and tousled hair.

"I'll help you look," he said gently and closed the door. "Where did you last see them?"

"Over there, by the vegetables. We were at that table," said Jenny pointing and slowly retracing her steps. She felt calmer now with the comforting presence of the tall stranger beside her.

Suddenly she heard a familiar voice call "Mummy!" and her heart leapt as Darren came running towards her from the direction of the rest house.

"Darren! Where have you been? Where's David?" cried Jenny, her voice shrill with relief.

"David is here" James's voice came through the darkness as he walked towards her holding David's hand.

"I stirred the pudding," said David proudly.

"We are cooks," said Darren quite unaware of the panic they had caused.

Jenny's face was radiant with relief as she looked at James. "They were in the kitchen, the cook was keeping them busy," he said.

"Oh thank you, I'll look after them better in future," said Jenny wondering what Richard would say if he knew that she had been so busy enjoying herself that she had not noticed where her children were.

She suddenly remembered the man beside her and turned to him shyly. "Thank you for helping. We must go home now," she said.

"So the rascals are found," called Sue coming towards them form the parked cars. "I should think you need a drink after all that worry."

"Oh no, we really must be going, it's getting late, the boys will be hungry."

"We're not hungry, the cook gave us some food," said Darren.

"Then please allow me to get you a drink," said the blonde-haired man addressing Jenny.

He looked closely at James. "It's James Patterson isn't it?" James looked puzzled then smiled. "George Farrier, hello. What are you doing in Bambo?"

They began walking towards the table.

"I 'm putting some cattle on the train to Munari."

"George has a farm out at Fort Joan," said James as they reached the table. "We met last year at an agricultural conference." He introduced everyone and George ordered a round of drinks and some crisps for the boys.

"Can we go back to the kitchen?" asked Darren.

Jenny looked uncertain.

"I'm sure it's okay," said George, "the cook is fond of children."

"Don't get lost," called Jenny as the boys scampered off.

"We weren't lost before!" shouted Darren.

"Have you lived in Chark long?" asked Larry turning to George.

George laughed, "All my life. I'm a Charkian."

"How big is your farm?" asked Sue.

"About five thousand hectares."

"What do you farm?" asked Hans.

"Mainly cattle. It's a good citrus area as well but transport is a problem so I just have a small orchard. I supply Fort Joan and the surrounding area."

"How do you transport the cattle? You are a long way form the abattoir or even the railway," observed Nelson. "In fact they are building an abattoir in Fort Joan but at the moment I have to bring the cattle by truck here then put them on the train. But as I am more interested in breeding than in producing beef cattle it is not so much of a problem."

He turned to James. "I can tell I'm in the company of teachers with all these questions."

"Oh we're not all teachers," he said.

"What do you do?" asked George looking at Jenny with interest.

"Me? Oh not a lot. I'm........." Jenny was about to say "I'm just the doctor's wife," then broke off feeling foolish. With a determined effort she said "I was a computer programmer before the boys were born."

"Really? I was wondering whether a computer would be useful to me for my accounts. Maybe you could show me how to use one. I'm afraid modern technology hasn't reached Fort Joan yet."

"I wish I'd brought mine with me. But I was so looking forward to leading a quiet life without the trappings of modern civilisation that I didn't think about it."

"And how is the quiet life?"

"Well it's not very quiet with Darren and David around and Richard rushing in and out and people knocking on the door all the time asking for the doctor. But I do enjoy my garden. It's so satisfying here because everything grows so quickly."

"Jenny's got a lovely garden," said Sue. " I'm afraid we're very lazy with ours and just employ someone to keep it tidy but Jenny's is really neat. And you've made a lot of improvements since you've been here Jenny."

"Do you get many people disturbing you?" asked Hans.

"Oh yes," said Jenny gaily. "All sorts of people come, there's no time to be bored."

She took a mouthful of beer and smiled confidingly at her companions. "Take last Sunday afternoon for instance. Richard had been called out and I was sitting in the house reading when there was a knock at the door. I got up and found an old man standing on the verandah waving a hospital card. I told him the doctor was out and he should go over to the hospital but he just stood there shouting at me and pointing at his card. He didn't look sick and I didn't know what to do. I tried to tell him again to go to the hospital but then he got really mad with me and he started to unbutton his shirt and thump his chest."

"Oh dear, what did you do?" asked Sue laughing.

Jenny grinned. "Well, I nearly asked Darren to let me borrow his stethoscope as the man obviously wanted me to examine him, but I thought he might realise I was a fraud. So I gave him a couple of aspirins!"

"And then he went away?" said George as everyone laughed.

"Well no, he wanted me to mark his card first!"

"And did you?" Nelson looked disapproving.

"Well, that was tricky I must admit. After studying the card for a bit I wrote the date then - to be seen by the doctor."

"That was clever," laughed George. "You must meet all sorts of people living at the hospital."

"Oh yes!" Jenny's face was flushed as she looked around at her audience. "There's a man who is brought in by his relatives when he goes berserk. He's quite a quiet man usually. I often see him sitting outside his compound when I'm walking to town. He always wears a battered old brown trilby. Well, every now and again he runs through the town stark naked except for the trilby. When his relatives catch him they bring him to the hospital where he's given sedatives and after a couple of days he's right as rain. He's no trouble at all as long as he's allowed to wear his trilby all the time. Well, there was a new ward sister on who didn't know about the trilby and she tried to make him take it off. He was very angry and jumped out of bed, tore off his hospital nightgown and ran out of the ward holding on to his hat. The sister, who is rather stout, chased after him with her little lace cap bobbing up and down as she ran. One of the patients joined in and by the time they ran past our gate there was our friend holding on to his trilby, the ward sister, the helpful patient puffing along in his dressing gown, a couple of nurses shrieking with laughter, a dog barking loudly, the Patel's gardener and Darren!"

Jenny paused to wipe the tears of laughter from her eyes as she recounted the tale.

"It looked as if they'd run straight out of the Little Gingerbread Man," she gasped.

"And what happened?" asked Sue wide-eyed.

"Sister Everett happened to be at home and quietly and calmly stepped in front of the man and he stopped. She took him by the arm and led him back to the ward."

Jenny emptied her glass with a flourish and beckoned the steward.

"My round!" she announced. "Same again for everyone?"
She caught sight of James looking at her reprovingly and she felt confused.

"It's getting late," he said. "We must be going."

"Oh James," said Sue, "we're having a party on Saturday at the dam. I hope you'll be able to come. It's our leaving party."

Jenny started, "you're not leaving are you!" she exclaimed.

"Not just yet but we've been given permission to go as soon as the exams are over as Larry's father is sick. So we thought we'd have the party beforehand."

She turned to George. "You're welcome to come too if you're still around."

"Thank you very much but I plan to be back in Fort Joan by then. But if anything brings me this way then I'd like to join you."

The steward coughed and looked at Jenny.

She bit her lip in embarrassment. It was obvious that James felt that it was time she went home and now that the gathering was breaking up she had no wish to stay. She looked at the steward then glanced away again wondering what to say.

"The lady would like you to bring her children," said George.

"Yes sir," said the steward and shambled off.

Jenny looked at George gratefully.

James put his cigarettes in his pocket and stood up.

"Thank you for the invitation, we'll try to make it. Goodnight everyone."

"Night," grunted Leintu as he followed.

"And now it's time I got these boys to bed," said Jenny getting up and steadying herself against the chair.

"Goodnight everybody. It's been nice meeting you," she said looking at George and then politely extending her smile to Nelson.

"Cheerio Jenny, drive safely. Cheerio boys," called Sue as the steward appeared at the door of the rest house with Darren and David.

"Goodnight! See you again soon!" called Darren taking David's hand and running towards his mother.

Chapter Six

Jenny glanced at the clouds scudding through the darkness and pressed the accelerator to the floor.

The excitement she had felt at the end of the evening was giving way to apprehension as she manoeuvred the car over the rough road away from the rest house. She was relieved when she reached the main road and, barely stopping at the junction, she swerved left and back towards the town.

"Mummy's driving fast!" screamed Darren in delight.

The sky lit up in front of them as a fork of lightning rent it in two.

"I want to get back before it rains," said Jenny as calmly as she could.

"Rain! rain! rain!" chanted Darren jumping up and down on the back seat.

"I want......." whimpered David, but his words were drowned by the clap of thunder that followed.

Jenny made an effort to slow down as they reached the town. She saw the hospital lights shining on the hill and drove more slowly still. She was beginning to feel slightly sick now. She was not used to drinking much especially on an empty stomach. She wished she knew what time it was but guessed guiltily that it was past the boys' bedtime.

"Hello Jonah!" shouted Darren to the nightwatchman as they drove through the hospital gates.

Jenny raised her hand to greet the old man and as she did so a dark shape obscured her vision. There was a sickening thud as the object hit the windscreen and bounced off the bonnet. Jenny braked abruptly throwing the children onto the floor. She glanced briefly to see that they were alright then opened the door and got out leaning unsteadily against the side of the car.

Jonah was backing away from a heap of feathers on the ground, his lips trembling and the whites of his eyes rolling in fear.

Jenny's heart started to beat faster as she stared with incomprehension at the nightwatchman's face.

"What is it?" she whispered.

The old man stumbled up to Jenny and grasped her shoulder. He shone his torch fleetingly at the creature and Jenny saw a trickle of blood oozing from its evil-looking beak. The bird's eye appeared to gleam malevolently in the unnatural light.

Jenny glanced behind and saw the scared faces of Darren and David peering out of the window.

"It's alright," she called with false gaiety. "We just hit a bird, that's all." She turned to open the car door.

"No!" hissed Jonah clutching Jenny again. His stale breath and the odour of his unwashed body enveloped her in a wave of nausea. She pushed the old man away, staggered forward and retched noisily.

He watched dispassionately then pointed to the dead bird. "Him owl," he said. "You kill owl. Owl bring bad luck." He spat on the ground.

"Oh," said Jenny nervously. She turned again and saw the white faces of her children pressed against the window. She started to walk towards the car but Jonah intercepted her.

"You kill owl," he growled. "You take him away. I no want him spirit here."

"Oh," said Jenny again. She looked about her helplessly. The old man stared at her, grunted and walked away. Jenny could see him shuffling in the darkness and muttering to himself as he appeared to be looking for something. After a few minutes he gave a grunt of satisfaction and returned to Jenny with a plastic bag.

"You put him in here," he said thrusting the bag at Jenny.

She walked slowly over to the owl and bent down. She laid the bag on the ground. It was only a little bit bigger than the bird.

"It's going to be a tight squeeze," she murmured weakly as she put out her hands to gather up the corpse.

The feathers were soft and the body still warm as she touched it.

Jenny recoiled in horror. Nausea threatened to overcome her again.

She became aware of the figure of Jonah standing grimly watching her and she fought back her feelings of revulsion. Quickly she picked up the owl, stuffed it in the bag, strode back to the car, opened the door and flung the thing on the floor by the passenger seat.

Only half conscious of what she was doing she wiped her hands on her skirt, flung herself into the driver's seat, slammed it into gear and drove off.

Fallen leaves, scraps of paper and a tin can danced along in front of them blown by the wind that heralded the approaching storm.

Jenny accelerated, then braked violently at the corner and accelerated again before coming to stop in a screech of brakes in the drive of the doctor's house.

The glare of the headlights picked up the figure of Richard running out of the house, his white coat open and flapping in the wind. Jenny noticed the stethoscope around his neck and realised that he must only have recently returned. She cursed herself inwardly for not having been back first; they probably would if it hadn't been for the owl. She shuddered as she caught sight of the bag on the floor.

"Where the hell have you been?" yelled Richard wrenching open the passenger door and scooping David up in his arms. Jenny noticed for the first time that his grubby face was streaked with tears. She looked anxiously at Darren but, although equally grubby, he showed no distress.

"We've been cooking and we killed an owl," he said in answer to his father's question.

"And here it is!" giggled Jenny hysterically waving the bag in Richard's face.

Richard glared at her. "You're drunk," he said coldly. Jenny fell back as if she had been hit.

"I'm not," she gasped. She looked up at the clean-shaven face of her husband. His lips were drawn into a tight, anxious line and he had dark rings under his eyes.

He's pushing himself too hard again, thought Jenny in a mixture of compassion and irritation.

A crack of thunder interrupted her thoughts.

"I have to bury this before it rains," she said. "You take the boys. I'll be in a minute."

Without waiting for an answer Jenny marched round to the back of the house, picked up a spade and thrust it into the earth. The ground was hard and she looked up at the sky longingly. We could do with some rain, she thought. She wondered whether to wait until the rain had softened the ground but she was anxious to get the job done straightaway. Sighing impatiently she picked up the bag and walked towards the water-melons, dragging the spade behind her. The earth was soft as she watered there every day. Quickly she dug a hole, thrust the owl to the bottom of it, shovelled earth on top and ran back to the house as the first drops of rain started to spatter on the ground.

Inside the house Richard was sitting on the settee reading a story to the boys. They were wearing their pyjamas and their faces were clean and shining.

Jenny gave a start of surprise. It was months since Richard had got the children ready for bed. She looked at him fondly as he said "And they all lived happily ever after." He closed the book and stood up.

Instinctively Jenny stepped forward, put her arms round him and kissed him. Richard moved aside and flung an embarrassed look at the children.

"You smell of beer," he hissed. He turned to the boys. "It's time for bed now," he said taking their hands and leading them past Jenny.

Jenny stood stunned, her face pale and her head swimming. She walked slowly to the kitchen, put on the kettle and sat down as she waited for it to boil. She caught sight of Richard's white coat flung over a chair and swallowed hard.

"You must be tired after working so late," she said as Richard appeared in the doorway.

"Yes I am," he said shortly. "I'm going to bed."

"But......," Jenny began, but Richard had already gone. Jenny sat watching the steam rising from the boiling kettle. The rain beat against the windows and she shivered violently. The kettle continued to boil and she was enveloped in a damp, protective haze. She slowly got up and made herself a cup of coffee. She held the mug in both hands and sat down again on the kitchen chair sipping the coffee and gently rocking backwards and forwards as she did so.

She shivered again.

It's a long time since I've been cold, she thought. Her mind wandered back to winter in England. It had been snowing the day she met Richard - hundreds of years ago it seemed. She and Pam had been climbing in Snowdonia with their mountaineering club. It had been the first time they had been in icy conditions and they had enjoyed the challenge of going up the Devil's Kitchen using ice picks and crampons. On their way down they had met a small party from one of the London medical schools. Jenny's party had felt quite superior as they watched the other group slithering about with no equipment. They had noted with gleeful horror that one of the girls was even wearing plimsolls. That night the two groups met again at the pub. Jenny had noticed Richard looking at her admiringly as she talked with animation about abseiling down Stannage Edge.

Jenny smiled softly to herself as she almost breathed again the atmosphere of the smoke-filled pub, heard the boisterous laughter and saw among the crowd a serious-looking young man with kind eyes watching her from behind his spectacles. He raised his glass of bitter and winked at her.

And that, thought Jenny, was how it all began. She looked at the empty cup in her hand and felt suddenly very tired. Mechanically she rinsed the cup and put it on the draining board.

She tiptoed along the passage to the boys' room. She stopped at the door for a moment listening to their regular breathing and her own breathing became calmer.

As she entered the room the curtain fluttered slightly but the storm was past now and the rain had almost stopped. Jenny went to Darren's bed and looked at him through the mosquito net. He had already kicked off his blanket but she did not want to disturb him and she knew it would get warmer once the rain had stopped. Lying there under the net he seemed vulnerable and yet she knew that as soon as he woke up the roles reversed and it was she who was suddenly vulnerable when faced with the explosive energy of a six-year old unchanneled by school, grandparents or peer group pressure.

Jenny sighed and turned slowly to look at David. He had rolled to the side of the bed and his face was pressed against the net, his distorted features making him look like a subnormal child. Jenny stood looking at him for a moment then she lifted the net and gently moved him to the middle of the bed. As she did so he gave a little cry and held out his arms to her. She kissed him gently, covered him with the sheet and tucked the mosquito net back into place.

When she reached her room and saw the inert body of
Richard lying uncompromisingly on his side of the bed
Jenny thought that she would never get to sleep.
She lay down watching jumbled images dance in front of
her before drifting into an uneasy sleep.
Jenny finds herself pushing her way through a crowd of
black people singing and dancing to the sound of drums.
They do not want to let her pass but she has to climb the
mountain which overshadows them. She shoves herself
through the throng and starts running, panting up the
mountain track but it soon disappears into loose scree.
The sun is pounding down on her and she has difficulty in
climbing because she is wearing ice crampons. She looks
back at the people. Now they are marching away from the
mountain and the drumbeats have changed to gunfire. The
mountain looms menacingly above her and she is quite
alone. Now she is near the top of the mountain and a
gentle wind is blowing in her face. She is walking along a
well-defined path at the edge of a precipice. The gunfire
has ceased and the solitude is overwhelming. Suddenly
she hears a bleat. She bends down and looks over the
precipice. Ten metres below a goat and her kid are
sheltering on a ledge. As Jenny watches, the image
changes. The goat has gone and the kid becomes David.
He is sleeping peacefully, his fair curls glinting in the sun.
A shadow passes over   the ledge and Jenny looks up to
see an eagle circling low, coming nearer and nearer the
sleeping child. David sits up and rubs his eyes, then opens
them wide in horror as he sees the approaching eagle, its
talons outstretched towards him. "David!" screams Jenny
and she feels herself tumbling over the precipice in her
effort to save him.
Frantically Jenny clawed at the bed as she awoke drenched
in sweat from her nightmare. It was empty. Hardly
conscious of what she was doing, she rushed along the
passage, switched on the boys' light and came to a stop by

David's bed. He was sleeping peacefully in the position she had left him. Slowly she turned to look at Darren. He too was still fast asleep under the mosquito net.

Her heart still beating loudly Jenny turned off the light and returned to her room. She fumbled for the bedside light, knocking the telephone as she switched it on. The jangle of the phone seemed to Jenny's overwrought nerves to echo through the house. She replaced the receiver and listened but there was no sound from the boys. She looked at the phone in bewilderment as she gazed at the empty bed. She hadn't heard it ring. Had she really been sleeping so soundly? Maybe it hadn't rung. Maybe Richard wasn't at the hospital. Where was he then? An image of the new sister of the casualty and out-patients department came into her mind. Sister Ningi had completed her training in England. She was an easy-going, self-confident woman in her mid-twenties with a rich voice and a playful smile that belied her professional approach to her work.

Jenny walked slowly to the door. Perhaps he's in the toilet, she thought in an effort to pull herself together. She padded along the passage to the bathroom but it was empty. She left the light on then went to the kitchen, dining room and finally the lounge.

She stood in the middle of the room looking around. There were some pieces of lego scattered on the grey tiled floor. A picture of a clown drawn by Darren hung from the wall suspended from one corner by a piece of blutack. Its upside down smile leered at her in a grotesque fashion. The three other pieces of blutack looked like gobs of chewing gum stuck to the wall. Not that it matters, thought Jenny looking around the once-white walls with distaste. The plaster was rough and the thinly-spread paint not washable. There was a black line a third of the way up the wall where the settee had rested before they moved the furniture round. The electric light, glaring from the middle of the ceiling, showed up a mosaic of smudges, scratches and fingerprints. Jenny caught sight of a fly suspended in a cobweb near the ceiling and frowned. Isaac had dusted the corners only the day before - these spiders certainly were diligent. Her glance rested on the desk in the corner of the room; copies of The Lancet were in a neat pile, a sombre-looking medical journal lay open and next to it a fountain pen rested on a notebook open at a page half-filled with Richard's precise handwriting. The top two shelves of the bookcase next to the desk were filled with neatly arranged medical books and journals. The bottom shelf was a haphazard collection of paperbacks and some library books lying on their side. I must take those back tomorrow, thought Jenny absently.

The rain had stopped and the atmosphere was already sticky and humid. She could hear the hum of insects outside and a mosquito sang insistently in her ear as she sank down into a chair. The steady sound of water dripping from the roof was overshadowed every now and then by a flurry from the flamboyant tree as it emptied its dripping branches in a gush upon the ground.

A sudden crack made Jenny leap up in fright. Then she sat down again foolishly realising that it was the tin roof expanding in the warmer air. The bathroom door swung slowly backwards and forwards creaking as it did so. Jenny wondered whether to get up and close it when she suddenly froze in terror. There was a rattle at the front door; someone was trying to get in. The flamboyant tree groaned and then all was quiet. Jenny, eyes transfixed on the door, realised that it was the wind playing tricks again. A moth fluttered around the light. It was small and nondescript and Jenny watched it with increasing irritation. She could never understand the self-destructive urge of these creatures. She thought of the owl lying at Jonah's feet and shuddered. She looked away but could still hear the moth's frantic death dance. Wearily she got up and pulled a chair under the light. She went to the kitchen and fetched a colander and a tea towel.

"I must be crazy," murmured Jenny as she hauled herself onto the chair and lifted the colander towards the flailing wings. She frowned in concentration as she attempted to rescue the moth.

The harsh light accentuated the lines on her forehead and made her skin look pallid.

Suddenly she heard footsteps outside and, still on the chair, she turned towards the door, her eyes popping in fear.

The door opened and Richard walked into the room then stood stock-still looking at Jenny in amazement.

"Where have you been?" she asked dropping the colander with a clatter.

"To the hospital of course. Where did you think I've been?"

"I didn't, didn't hear the phone," said Jenny feebly getting off the chair.

"I'm not surprised, you were in that much of a stupor," retorted Richard. He looked around angrily. "And why are all the lights on?"

"I had a bad dream," whispered Jenny.

"Well I've had a bad reality," said Richard glaring at her from behind his glasses.

"Yes; the accident. You never told me about it. Let me make you some coffee."

"I've already had some." He strode to the kitchen and switched off the light. "I'm going back to bed," he said as he clicked off the dining room light.

"I'll come too," said Jenny, but she remained where she was as she listened to Richard purposefully switching off the bathroom, passage and bedroom lights.

I wonder who made him coffee, frowned Jenny as she stooped to pick up a piece of paper lying on the floor. She turned it over and saw a mountain scene with Happy

Birthday printed at the top. She smiled ruefully and put it back on the mantelpiece.

Pam's had been the only birthday card she had received.

Anyway, she thought wearily remembering Larry's generous attempt to order champagne, it was a nice evening.

Slowly she got up and followed Richard to the bedroom.

Chapter Seven

The moth was nowhere to be seen the next morning but the chair in the middle of the room and the tea towel and colander on the floor made Jenny realise sinkingly that only some of the events of the previous night had been a dream.

Slowly she picked up the things and replaced the chair. She stood for a moment looking, unseeing, out of the window and wondering what to do. It was seven o'clock and Richard should be on duty at half past. However, he was still sleeping soundly and Jenny knew he needed the rest. She went to the kitchen and put the kettle on to boil still undecided. It seemed a pity to wake Richard especially as the boys were still asleep.

Jenny stood waiting for the kettle to boil then she automatically made two cups of coffee. Well, I might as well give it to him, she thought as she stirred powdered milk into Richard's mug. She carried it to the bedroom but he was still fast asleep. "Here's your coffee," she said softly putting it beside the phone.

She took hers outside and sat on the verandah. The sky was a cloudless blue and the leaves had a freshly-washed look after last night's storm. Many of the seed pods from the flamboyant tree had been blown down and were scattered on the grass. A lizard scurried along the path then stopped, its throat pulsating as it waited otherwise motionless for an unsuspecting insect to land within its reach.

Jenny sipped her coffee enjoying the precious minutes on her own. If the boys slept a bit longer she could write and thank Pam for her birthday card. There had not been a letter with it and Jenny wondered when she was coming. She stretched out her legs and thought about her friend. It would be so good to see her again. She was really looking forward to the trip north they planned to take when Pam came.

Feeling refreshed by the early morning sunshine Jenny went back into the house and set up her type-writer on the table in the dining room. She was soon absorbed in a light-hearted description of her visit to the rest house the previous evening.

Smiling to herself as the keys clattered in the type-writer Jenny was hardly aware of the phone ringing. She looked up suddenly to see Richard looking angrily down at her as he buttoned his shirt.

"Why didn't you wake me ?" he demanded. "It's eight o'clock and they need me in theatre."

As Jenny looked at her husband's agitated face she felt all the energy draining out of her. She got up, carefully pushing the chair back in its place.

"I'm sorry, I thought you needed the rest. I'll make you a fresh cup of coffee."

"I haven't time to sit around drinking coffee," he shouted pulling on his white coat.

"But Richard you can't go without any breakfast. And anyway, anyway......." Jenny tailed off uncertainly.

"Anyway what?"

Jenny shrugged. She wanted to tell him about the owl, about the conversation between Leintu, James and Nelson, about losing the boys, and she suddenly desperately wanted to tell him about her nightmare.

"Well?" Richard moved towards the door.

"What time will you be back?" asked Jenny lamely.

"When I have attended to my cases," he replied stiffly as he walked out of the door.

"Goodbye then," said Jenny but he was already hurrying down the path.

She heard the gate click and was surprised to feel tears pricking her eyelids.

"Good morning madam."

Jenny turned and saw Isaac standing at the kitchen door. "Oh good morning Isaac. Come in," she said brightly. "The boys are still asleep."

"No matter madam. I polish lounge floor first."

Jenny sighed. Of course; it was Wednesday. Isaac followed his own strict routine and on a Wednesday he took all the furniture from the lounge and dining room outside then washed and polished the floors. Jenny had tried to tell him that it wasn't necessary but he had just smiled and said that he always did it that way when he worked for Mrs. Ferguson. Sometimes Jenny felt as she looked around at the tatty government furniture that she had no control over anything. And certainly not my children, she thought as Darren and David came tumbling into the room shouting at each other.

"Boys! Not first thing in the morning. Shut up!"

"But he's got my car," said David reproachfully.

"You had my book."

"I was only looking at the pictures."

Jenny felt a wave of hatred surge through her. She caught sight of Isaac's kindly face observing the boys with detached tolerance and said briskly, "Come and have some breakfast."

As Jenny sat watching her sons crunching their toast she wondered what they should do with the day stretching out ahead of them. She knew she and Darren should do some school-work but she did not feel she could face the battle that would probably ensue. David was now becoming increasingly demanding when she was working with Darren and was not content to draw or paint on his own. She knew she should make more effort to find playmates for them but it wasn't easy.

"What are we going to do today?" demanded Darren as he noisily drained his glass of milk.

"What would you like to do?" Jenny threw the question back.

"See the trains," said David.

Jenny sighed. "Okay then, we'll see the trains."

Bambo station was little more than a halt on the line running between Munari and Mutape and then through Tambalia until it reached the coast. The single line track had been built nearly a hundred years ago and it was in need of constant repair.

The station was situated on the edge of the town on the road going out to join the main Munari-Mutape road. It was not somewhere they went often because, apart from the fact that Jenny found it boring, it was a long walk from the hospital. Previously they had made a detour to look at the trains - if there were any - when they had taken the car. Some perverse instinct had made Jenny decide to walk that morning and by the time they arrived the sun was already high and they were all hot and tired.

There was a goods train standing at the station and Jenny was surprised to see that the place was a hive of activity. The wooden kraal at the end of the platform was filled with cattle and the train was carefully positioned so that half a dozen cattle trucks were adjacent to it.

Jenny and the boys walked across the station yard to get a better look. The kraal was divided into sections and leading from the exit was a strongly-fenced passage, the width of a large cow, going to the railway line. A steep wooden ramp joined the end of the passage with the door of a cattle truck. Several men brandishing sticks were attempting to get a large brown cow from the ramp into the truck. It kept kicking wildly and trying to move backwards but two more cows were waiting in the passage behind it. They too tried to move backwards but a strong pole had been put at the back to block their retreat.

The commotion had attracted a crowd of on-lookers as well as the owners of the cattle and the station officials who were attempting to organise the operation.

"There's that man we saw last night," said Darren.

"Which man?" Jenny pretended to look around but she had already noticed George's blonde hair amongst the crowd. From the way he was acting it seemed that the cattle being loaded were his. Jenny lifted David on her shoulders and Darren scrambled through people's legs to get a better view.

"Careful Darren!" called Jenny thinking of the lashing hooves but he was already standing at the front of the crowd.

She watched in fascination as the brown cow gave an angry bellow and then charged up the ramp and into the truck. One of the officials conferred with George and wrote something on a form attached to his clip-board. The men then started persuading the two cattle in the passage to follow suit. They were less stubborn than the first cow and did what was required of them without too much trouble. The door of the truck was then slammed closed and the train shunted forward so that an empty cattle wagon was next to the ramp.

The official with the clip-board handed it to George who studied the form, nodded in agreement, wrote something and handed it back.

George then started making his way through the crowd pausing now and again to speak to someone. When he reached Jenny he smiled with pleasure.

"Hello. What brings you here?"

Jenny suddenly felt out of place amidst the bellowing cattle and sweating bodies. She wondered if George thought she had been spying on him and found herself speechless with embarrassment.

At that point Darren reappeared chattering excitedly and Jenny lifted David down next to him.

"The boys wanted to see the trains. I didn't expect to find such an exciting spectacle though," she said and stepped back hurriedly as a large cow broke loose and stampeded across the station yard. "It must be hard work loading them in this heat," she added.

"Yes it is," said George his face glowing with exertion. "Thirsty work too. I expect you'd like a drink after standing in the sun?"

Jenny hesitated. "Well, thank you, that would be very nice."

George led the way to a small building ostentatiously bearing the name Station Hotel. There were a couple of benches on the roughly-made verandah. The interior of the building appeared dark in contrast to the glare outside. Half the room they stepped into served as a shop selling a small selection of food and the other half was set out with chairs and tables.

"What would you like to drink?" asked George as they approached the counter.

"Oh, anything cold," said Jenny diffidently.

"Beer?"

"Oh no, no thank you."

George smiled at the girl behind the counter. "Three cokes and one beer," he said in Chakari. "Shall we have it here or outside?" he added turning to Jenny.

Jenny looked at the flies buzzing around the poorly washed tables and at a fat cockroach scurrying across the floor.

"Outside would be nicer I think," she replied tactfully.

"So, you boys get about don't you?" said George as he opened the cans and handed them to Darren and David. They just grinned and gulped their drinks. David let out a loud burp and both boys chortled delightedly.

Jenny looked pained but before she could say anything George asked, "How long have you been in Bambo?"

"Just over a year and a half. We came the September before last."

"And do you like it here?"

Jenny thought for a moment. "When we first came it was all very new and interesting. I started to learn Chakari and made one or two friends in town." Jenny found herself telling George about Mrs. Ntoo and her family.

"That's nice for you to have a friend like that, and nice for her too."

"Yes, I suppose so. It just seems rather superficial that's all. I sometimes take her a cake and we sit in her compound and drink tea. We don't say very much because my Chakari isn't very good but I enjoy being there and its nice for Darren and David to play with the children. Sometimes she gives us sugar cane to take home and the boys really like that."

"I wouldn't call that superficial," said George gravely. "I've known expatriates in Munari who don't allow their servants to even drink a cup of tea in the house. And very few would make the effort to visit people in their own homes."

"Maybe," said Jenny uncertainly, "but they never call in on me."

"And they would never call in on the chief either. Don't forget, you're the doctor's wife and the doctor's house is somewhere that they would visit only in great emergency." Jenny sighed. "So the doctor's wife and children have to suffer."

George looked at her quizzically. "Have you travelled much in Chark?" he asked.

"No. My friend from England is coming next month and we plan to see the north then. Richard has applied for a week's leave but I'm hoping he'll be able to take some overtime as well because I'd like to have some time in the Vandu Mountains."

"The Vandu Mountains," said George reflectively. "Yes, you'll enjoy the mountains. They've got a wild beauty about them. Parts of them are really inhospitable but other parts are more inviting. There's a beautiful waterfall that's not too far off the beaten track. And some interesting caves." George gazed into the distance as if he were looking, not at a small dusty railway station, but at mountain peaks on the far horizon. He turned to Jenny. "My farm looks out on to the western edge of the range. Where were you thinking of staying?"

"According to the map there's a small town on the eastern slopes about two hundred kilometres from Mutape. I thought we might be able to stay there for a day or two."

"That'll be Yonda. It's a pretty little place, fairly isolated but there's a self-catering rest house there."

George looked thoughtfully at Jenny. "Why don't you make it a round trip? The rains will have stopped by then and the road through the mountains will be passable. If you made an early start you could easily be at Rossano in a day."

"Rossano?"

"That's the name of my farm."

"Oh. It sounds Italian."

"Yes it is. My grandfather married the daughter of an Italian farmer who came out to Africa in the gold rush days. He used the money he made to start up a small vineyard on the slopes of the Vandu and he named it after his home town."

"That sounds very romantic. Do you really own a vineyard?"

George laughed. "No, the vineyard was never a success. It's too hot and there's not enough rain to produce grapes commercially although some of the original vines are still there. When my grandfather took over the farm he started cattle breeding and that's the main source of income."

Jenny's face flushed with excitement. "I'd love to see the farm. But wouldn't we be rather a crowd?"

"Oh there's plenty of room," George paused, "now that there's only me at home."

Jenny looked at him questioningly and saw a look of unfathomable sadness on his face.

"My father died nearly four years ago," he said as if in explanation.

Jenny's murmur of regret was drowned by the shriek from the whistle and clanging of wagons as the train shunted further along the line.

"I'm hungry," announced David.

Jenny glanced at her watch. "Gracious, it's nearly lunch time. Daddy will be home soon. That is," she paused remembering Richard hurrying from the house at the beginning of the morning, "unless he's not too busy."

"Where's your car?" George looked around.

"We walked."

"You walked?" There was admiration as well as surprise in his voice. "Well it's too hot to walk now." He turned to the boys. "How would you kids like a ride in a cattle truck?"

"Ooh yes!" they cried jumping up and running across the yard to the white truck parked by the siding.

Darren and David waved excitedly as the truck slowed down at the hospital gates and finally came to a halt outside their house.

"Would you like some lunch?" asked Jenny as George helped them to get out.

"Are you sure it's no trouble?"

"Not at all. And anyway I'd like you to meet Richard."

"Well thank you." George switched off the engine and jumped lightly down slamming the door behind him.

When they entered the house Jenny saw that Isaac had laid only three places at the table. "Where's Doctor North?" she asked.

"He have no time for lunch, madam. He just have a quick sandwich then he go."

Jenny sighed. "Okay, well can you lay another place for Mr. Farrier please?"

She turned to George, "Please make yourself at home. I'll just put some things on the table."

"That lettuce looks nice," said George as they sat down. "Did you grow it?"

"Yes, it was a good crop this time. The last lot got eaten by ants. Do help yourself. Darren, please keep your mouth shut when your eating."

Jenny cut up the tomato on David's plate. "When are you leaving?" she asked not looking at George.

"I plan to make an early start tomorrow. The vehicle is getting old and the road won't be very good after last night's rain but I should be in Fort Joan before dark."

"Do you come to Bambo very often?" Jenny heard herself ask, her voice sounding unnaturally bright.

George looked at her across the table. "No," he said. Then added, "But I'll be passing through again in a couple of weeks on my way to Munari." He hesitated for a few moments. "Perhaps I could call in then and see if you are still interested in staying at my farm when your friend comes."

"That's very kind of you. I'll see what Richard says. David, what are you doing?" she finished as she suddenly caught sight of David dipping his knife into the mayonnaise. As he transferred it to his plate drips of yellow liquid landed on the freshly laundered cloth. He looked at Jenny shamefaced and in his confusion licked the rest of the mayonnaise off the knife.

"I could kill them sometimes," said Jenny quietly. She got up. "Would you like some coffee?"

"Are you making some for yourself? I don't want to detain you."

"No, it's nice to have someone to talk to. Now David, if you've finished you can get down but don't sit there playing with your food."

"Come David, let's play outside," said Darren sensing his mother's rising irritation.

"Perhaps you'd like to sit on the verandah while I make the coffee," suggested Jenny.

"Is there anything I can do to help?"

"No, it won't take a minute and Isaac will wash the dishes."

Jenny carried the tray with the coffee out to the verandah and for a moment they sat in silence.

They caught a glimpse of red as a small bishop bird flew into the garden and then away again. The milkweed bush was beginning to drop its flowers and the lawn was scattered with yellow trumpets.

"It's peaceful here," said George.

"Sometimes. Not always though. We're a bit too near the hospital."

George smiled. "Ah yes, madmen and barking dogs." He took a sip of coffee. "I hope you got back before the storm yesterday evening."

"Only just. George," Jenny looked at him earnestly, "are owls really evil?"

"Owls?" George looked startled. "Well of course in western literature owls are portrayed as wise old birds but in Africa people really do believe that they are portents of evil. Why do you ask?"

Jenny told George about the incident the previous night.

"That must have been most upsetting for you," said George his face full of concern.

Jenny felt confused, she had half expected him to laugh at her.

"Yes. I couldn't sleep. And when I did I had a dream." Jenny was horrified to suddenly find tears coursing down her cheeks.

"Tell me about it."

Haltingly Jenny recounted the dream. Her memory was already managing to blot it out and she had difficulty piecing it together. When she finished she felt very tired but more relaxed than she had all day.

"Thanks for listening," she said shyly looking up at George's tanned face.

"It's easier if you can share things," he said. He looked at his watch. "Well, I suppose I'd better be going. I'm sorry I didn't meet your husband."

"I'll tell him about your invitation. And we'll see you in a couple of weeks?"

George looked at her steadily for a moment. "Yes, I'll be back," he said.

Chapter Eight

"But Richard, Larry and Sue have been our friends for nearly two years, they would be very hurt if we didn't go to their leaving party."

It was Friday evening, the boys were in bed and Jenny and Richard were sitting on the verandah. Richard irritably slapped a mosquito that had settled on his arm. "I don't want to waste my time with a load of teachers. Why don't we go to the rest house and have that meal we missed on Tuesday?"

Jenny looked non-plussed. "You mean for my birthday treat?"

"Yes."

"Well actually I think I'd rather go to the party."

Richard looked hurt and Jenny realised she had said the wrong thing.

"There's no reason why we couldn't do both," she said quickly. "Go to the party on Saturday and out for a meal one evening next week."

"Come now, we don't want to go wild," said Richard smiling a little.

Jenny smiled back with relief. The tension that had hung around the house for the last few days was beginning to evaporate. The sudden arrival of the new Egyptian doctor the day after the bus accident had made Jenny more optimistic about the future.

"Are you on call this week-end?"

"On Sunday but Dr. Fatti's in on Saturday."

"What's he like to work with?"

"It's a bit early to say," said Richard cagily. "What's his wife like?"

"She seemed pleasant although I only met her for a few minutes the day after they arrived. I called again to invite her round but she was visiting the Egyptian family at the secondary school. I'm sure........" finished Jenny then bit her tongue.

"Sure what?"

"Oh nothing." She had been going to say that she was sure she had told Richard that before but she did not want to spoil the atmosphere.

"Shall we go tomorrow? The boys would enjoy it," pressed Jenny.

"Well if you really want to," said Richard with as good a grace as he could manage.

"And what about our trip through the mountains to Fort Joan?" Jenny was longing to ask but felt that this wasn't the time. Richard had been reticent when she had first mentioned it and she thought she would wait a few days before referring to it again.

"Shall I make some coffee?" she asked instead.

Richard glanced at his watch. "I just want to go and check the patient whose appendix I removed this morning. I'll have some when I come back." He got up. "I won't be long. I promise."

"Okay Doctor," said Jenny with forced gaiety, "your coffee will be served in exactly fifteen minutes."

"Will there be party games?" asked Darren excitedly the following afternoon as the Beetle bounced over the rough road leading to the dam.

"I don't know. But there'll probably be other children to play with," replied Jenny.

"They've got a pleasant day for it anyway," remarked Richard at the wheel. "Cool enough and with little likelihood of rain." He was looking less tired now although the tension lines on his forehead were still there.

"There's the dam!" shouted David as they turned a corner. They looked out on to a wide expanse of grass going down to the edge of a small lake, blue and sparkling in the sunshine. One end of the lake was dammed by a crude, though efficient, earth wall. The other end got progressively smaller until it tapered into the original river. The land on the other side of the lake rose quite steeply for a couple of hundred feet.

"There's not a lot of shade to park under," said Richard.

"It doesn't matter, it's not hot and anyway it'll be dark by the time we leave."

Richard looked startled, "Dark?"

"It gets dark by six o'clock these evenings," Jenny reminded him patiently.

"Well, we'll just park next to this Peugeot," said Richard pulling up next to Hans's car. He looked around with relief. "There don't seem to be many people here."

"Hello!" said Sue coming towards them. "You're the first to arrive. Would like a drink?"

"Oh not yet thanks. What can we do to help?"

"I think we've got everything under control," Sue nodded at Larry and Hans who were just putting the grid on to the fire they had made. There was a pile of wood beside it and a couple of tables with boxes of food on them.

Beside the tables were two tin baths filled with canned drinks being kept cold by large blocks of ice.

"We brought a couple of folding chairs," said Richard opening the boot.

"That's great. We've got quite a few now and some rugs and cushions as well. Moses will be here soon. He'll be bringing some of the teachers in his truck and also the music. He runs the discos at school and he's got a great selection of tapes."

"It sounds as if it's going to be quite a party," said Jenny not looking at Richard.

"We've invited about sixty people but I don't know if they'll all come. Oh look, here's Mr. Mapilo with his family. Now you'll have some friends to play with boys." A brown Ford Cortina that had obviously seen better days parked next to the North's and the principal of the secondary school got out. He was short and stocky, very black, and had a charming smile.

"Hello Sue, is it alright if I leave my family? I've got some business to attend to, I'll collect them later."

"No that's fine," she said and smiled at Mrs. Mapilo as she got out. She was taller and lighter-complexed than her husband. Her reserved manner and elegant appearance made Jenny feel slightly unkempt in her comfortable sandals and cotton dress that had once been brightly coloured but was now faded from being repeatedly hung out to dry in the harsh sun.

Mr. Mapilo opened the back door and four smartly dressed children stepped shyly out. The eldest boy was about ten, then came a girl a year or two younger and two more of similar ages to Darren and David.

"Hello Doctor, hello Mrs. North, see you later," Mr. Mapilo waved as he hurriedly got back into the car and drove off.

"Have you met Mrs. Mapilo?" asked Sue.

Jenny was about to say no but Richard said earnestly, "Yes I know Sister Mapilo. You run the clinic at Mooka don't you?"

Mrs. Mapilo inclined her head slightly and murmured that she did.

"Well you two have something to talk about. Would you like to sit down?" Sue led the way towards Larry and Hans at the fire.

"I think it's time we all had a drink," said Larry after they had greeted the new arrivals.

The children stood eyeing each other up and down as they solemnly drank from their cans. When they had finished the eldest boy looked at Darren and said, "Come!" then set off towards the water's edge.

"Don't go in," cautioned Sue. "There's bilharzia in the water."

Darren looked enquiringly at his parents. "You can go and play but not in the water," said Jenny.

"They should be happy for a while anyway," said Sue as the six children ran off.

Jenny smiled at her friend. "I shall miss you," she said.

"We're going to miss being here, it's a pity we've got to rush back. But I thought you were leaving in September?"

Jenny glanced at Richard deep in conversation with Mrs. Mapilo. "We haven't decided yet. Richard feels he's needed and I think he'd like to stay."

"And you?"

"I don't know. It's different for him, and for you too. You've got your work but I haven't any raison d'etre as it were."

"Sorry?"

Jenny gazed across the water and watched a hawk circling and then come slowly to land on a rocky crag. "Don't you sometimes wish you could leave everything and fly away like a bird?"

Sue smiled at her uncertainly. "Well......"

"And anyway," interrupted Jenny, "I don't think I can stand another year of being cooped up with the boys. Darren must go to school. But I don't think the local one here is suitable."

"I'm sure it will work out," said Sue hesitantly then brightened as a pick-up rounded the corner and roared across the grass.

The place suddenly burst into life as Moses, Nelson and a couple of other young male teachers jumped out of the vehicle. They were joined by three other men who Jenny vaguely recognized but was unable to place. All were dressed casually in brightly-coloured open-necked shirts. One of them seemed considerably taller than the rest, his long thin legs gave Jenny the impression he was walking on stilts and his Afro hairstyle framed his face like a halo. Jenny was not able to catch everyone's name as they were introduced but she gave a gasp of amused surprise as the tall man shook her hand and, smiling engagingly, told her his name was Tallboy.

Soon cans were being opened and the music was set up amidst lots of laughter and contradictory instructions.

A couple of other cars arrived filled to the brim with both men and women. Jenny caught a look of surprise on Sue and Larry's faces as they were introduced to some of the people who were obviously strangers, but everyone was made to feel welcome. Some people started to dance and Jenny found her feet tapping as she moved across to talk to Richard and Mrs. Mapilo.

"It's very generous of Larry and Sue to invite so many people," observed Richard as another Beetle followed by a land-rover arrived. An Indian teacher and his family got out of the Beetle and a middle-aged white couple came towards them from the land-rover.

"I don't think we've met. I'm Abe Jefferson and this is my wife Pearl. We're from the United States," shouted the man genially above the noise of the music.

"Do you live in Bambo?" asked Jenny looking at the couple in surprise. The man was short, on the stout side and balding. Despite his expansive smile his eyes had a cold determination about them that made Jenny nervous. In contrast, his wife had an angular appearance but her mouth as well as her eyes showed the same quality of single-mindedness as her husband.

"No, we're from Song," replied Pearl briskly. She looked around at the carefree crowd and passed her hand through her severely-cut grey hair in some bewilderment.

"You have come far," observed Mrs. Mapilo quietly. "How is the road?"

"There were one or two bad patches after last week's rain but the journey only took three hours as usual."

"What do you do out there?" asked Richard.

"We're missionaries. We run a small Bible school where we train pastors."

Jenny, Richard and Mrs. Mapilo listened politely as the couple told them of their efforts to train Charkians to take the word of the Lord into the remotest villages.

Suddenly Richard jumped up. "Good Lord!" he said, not noticing the pained expression on Pearl's face as he interrupted. "There's Dr. Fatti!"

Jenny followed his gaze and saw Dr. Fatti and his wife join the party with the Egyptian couple from the secondary school. The doctor was a good-looking man a little older than Richard. He was wearing an expensive-looking tropical suit in pale pink and, despite the fact that he was a little overweight, he cut a striking figure as he escorted his wife through the crowd to greet Larry and Sue. Mrs. Fatti's low-cut black dress, crystal jewellery and carefully-coiffured hair caused the dancers to stop and stare admiringly.

Richard however was not impressed. "He's meant to be on duty!" he said in an agitated whisper.

Jenny put her hand on his arm. "There's nothing you can do about it," she said firmly.

"But supposing there's an emergency?"

"Maybe he told them where he was."

"But he can't do that."

Jenny sighed and looked at the couple with admiration. "He just has."

She looked towards the fire. "It looks as if they're ready to start cooking the meat. I'll see if they need any help."

As she got up a cattle truck appeared round the corner and drove towards the other vehicles.

Jenny stared in disbelief as she recognized George at the wheel. She found herself flushing in pleasure and confusion and then, as she realised what she was doing, carried on walking nonchalantly towards the fire.

"Hello Jenny," George had caught her up and was smiling at her.

Jenny looked into his friendly, open face and relaxed. "Hello, it's nice to see you, but I thought you were going home on Thursday?"

"I started out but I had a break-down sixty kilometres down the road. I tried to fix it but discovered I needed a new fuel pump so I hitched back into Bambo but there wasn't one here so I had to wait until one was sent by train from Munari. I got it fixed this morning. I was wondering whether to leave this afternoon and drive through the night when I met Larry at the petrol station and he persuaded me to come to the party."

"That's great. And it means you can meet Richard," said Jenny turning back in the direction she had come from.

Richard was still upset about Dr. Fatti and was rather preoccupied when Jenny introduced George. Jenny reminded him of George's invitation and he looked surprised but nodded vaguely saying that they ought to see more of the country.

When they heard he was from Fort Joan, Pearl and Abe asked after some missionary friends in the area. George was in the middle of giving what news he had of them when the children arrived chattering excitely in a mixture of English and Charkian about what they had been doing. The Mapilo children had lost their newly-scrubbed look and Jenny glanced at their mother to see what she thought about it but she was smiling tranquilly and listening to them all.

"The kids must have smelt the food," said Sue as she approached. "Would you all like to come and get something to eat?"

Richard looked worried. "Thanks very much, then I think we'll have to go."

Sue raised her eyebrows in surprise and Richard explained that there was no doctor at the hospital and that he was worried about his appendix case. Sue looked at Jenny sympathetically and suggested that she and the boys stayed on and got a lift back later.

Richard bit his lip anxiously and looked towards the group of people drinking and dancing. "But will you be able to get a lift in time for the boys' bedtime?"

"I don't suppose Mrs. Mapilo plans to stay late with her children," said Jenny trying to keep the irritation from her voice, "we'll come back with them. If that's alright," she added smiling at Mrs. Mapilo.

Richard looked relieved. "Well, in that case I think I'll go now." He quickly said goodbye and was gone.

Jenny had been aware of George standing silently during this exchange; she wondered what he had been thinking but it was impossible to tell as Abe had begun asking him about his farm.

Mrs. Mapilo stood up and Jenny walked with her and the children towards the fire. The sun had sunk behind the hills and the water now looked black and cold and the crags rose starkly above the lake.

Once among the crowd around the fire Jenny's feeling of irritation vanished and she joined a group she knew. There was a lull in the dancing while everyone ate and replenished their drinks. Gradually people drifted back into the area they had improvised as a dance floor and Jenny watched them wistfully, her feet tapping to the beat. Most of the men were dancing on their own quite uninhibited by the lack of a partner. A couple of Charkian girls wearing tight jeans were also dancing together and Jenny was just wondering whether to join them when she felt a hand on her shoulder.

"Would you care to dance?" said a husky, unmistakably African voice in her ear.

Jenny spun round and found herself face to face with James. His sudden appearance unnerved her and she stared for a moment watching the firelight chase shadows across his face, his expression melancholy as he held her gaze.

"We've just arrived," he said briefly nodding towards Leintu who was gnawing at a chicken bone and talking in an over-loud voice to Tallboy and a group of other young men. Nelson appeared to be saying something but Leintu waved him aside dismissively, his large bulk dominating the group.

Jenny noticed a look of irritation mixed with something like fear flash across James's face as he looked at Leintu smiling provokingly at the group surrounding him.

"Come," he said imperiously grabbing Jenny's hand and pulling her into the middle of the dancers. The music was loud and the tempo fast and Jenny abandoned herself to the rhythm, propelled by the demonic energy of her partner. Time seemed to stand still, Jenny was aware of nothing except her body twisting, swaying, writhing in time to the music and mirroring her partner as they danced in unison circling each other but never touching.

Gradually the other dancers fell back to give them space and Jenny was dimly aware of their clapping. Someone improvised a drum and the drumbeat and the clapping matched her heartbeat. Jenny glanced up and saw that the moon had risen, she raised her arms upwards towards it as if in supplication, the clapping became louder and the spectators started to stamp. Jenny looked towards the dark faces surrounding her but could only make out the grim white face of Pearl Jefferson, her steely eyes fixed on Jenny's gyrating body in contempt. She faltered momentarily and looked at James but he hadn't noticed. His eyes were glazed and he was dancing like one possessed. Jenny knew that he was no longer aware of her and her legs suddenly felt like lead. She looked wildly round at the stamping crowd and her earlier elation turned to panic as she had visions of being forced to dance all night.

Then she saw through the shadows a tall blonde figure striding towards the record player. The music stopped. She remained still for a moment letting the silence envelop her like a protective mantle.

Then slowly and with dignity Jenny left the circle. Someone called out to her but she did not hear.

The music started up again and as people resumed their dancing her only thought was to get away from the crowd. A shaft of moonlight was shining across the lake and, hardly knowing what she did, Jenny made her way towards it. She reached the edge of the lake and stared down at the water lapping against the shore. A gentle breeze wafted over her face bringing with it smells of smoke and grilled meat mingled with the warm and subtle scents of the African night. Her pulse rate had returned to normal and although some of the exhilaration of the dance remained, her fear had gone.

She did not hear the footsteps on the grass until they were right behind her but she felt neither fear nor surprise when she half-turned and saw George, his face full of concern as he looked at her.

"Isn't it beautiful," said Jenny simply indicating the moonlight in the water.

"Yes," answered George.

As he stood beside her Jenny felt his steady strength and was comforted. She slipped her arm through his and they stood for a while companionably looking out across the lake.

A sudden shout from the merry-makers made Jenny start guiltily.

"The boys...........?" she faltered.

"They're fine. They were too busy playing with the Mapilo children to take any notice of the dancing," said George in reply to Jenny's unspoken question.

Another shout was heard followed by several angrier ones.

"I wonder what's going on?" said Jenny

"It looks like a disagreement about something," replied
George as they turned to make out the overpowering figure
of Leintu bearing down on Nelson.

The shouting became louder, there was a squeal from
Nelson, then they made out the lanky figure of Tallboy
jumping between them, his fist aimed at Leintu's jaw.
Leintu ducked and Nelson ran off wildly towards the lake
clutching his ear and shouting obscenities as he went.
Leintu started to follow him but was restrained by Moses.
Jenny held her breath as she watched Leintu grapple with
both Moses and Tallboy then break free and come hurtling
towards them in pursuit of Nelson.

As soon as he realised he was being followed Nelson
veered away from the water and ran in the direction of the
dam wall.

"What's he doing?" whispered Jenny as they watched the
small figure clamber up on the wall and start to run across
the dam.

"I don't think he knows," said George.

There was a roar from Leintu as he too reached the dam
and leapt up and along the wall gaining rapidly on Nelson.
Moses and Tallboy, closely followed by James, stood
watching and shouting a mixture of instructions, pleas and
threats. They were soon joined by others who had left the
dancing and run toward the dam anxious not to miss
anything.

A gasp went up from the crowd as Leintu got hold of
Nelson and shook him roughly by the shoulders. Still
spitting out obscenities Nelson managed to wriggle free
and viciously kneed his adversary in the groin. A shriek
echoed across the lake as Leintu doubled up in pain. At
this Nelson jumped up and down cackling wildly. Leintu
made a feeble grab for him but he stepped just out of reach
and continued to dance up and down chanting mockingly.
Slowly Leintu straightened himself up and advanced

purposefully towards the taunting figure in front of him. Both men were oblivious to the calls from their friends. Jenny caught sight of James looking strained and strangely isolated in the crowd.

Leintu made a sudden lunge forward, Nelson stepped sideways to avoid the blow, lost his balance and tumbled with a blood-curdling cry into the water below.

Jenny gave a scream and started to tremble uncontrollably. "It's a good thing he went over that side," said George putting his arm around her shoulder. "He could have smashed his head on the rocks the other side."

"But do you think he can swim?" stammered Jenny as they watched the angry figure floundering in the water.

"Good God! He probably can't!" George ran towards the water. Then hesitated as a slim figure raced along the dam wall and dived in, surfacing next to Nelson. It was James. George stood at the edge of the water for a moment watching as James attempted to grip Nelson under the armpits and tow him to shore. Nelson, however, oblivious of the fact that he was in danger of drowning, was using all his strength to fight James off. The silhouettes of the men struggling in the water suddenly vanished as the moon slid behind a cloud plunging everything into inky blackness. Quickly George kicked off his sandals and strode into the water in the direction of the splashing. Jenny heard him swimming strongly, the splashing increased then died down as between them George and James brought the limp body of Nelson towards the shore.

Once they reached the shallow water Nelson stood upright, spluttered and weakly but determinedly shook himself free of his rescuers.

"Ntisi swine," he hissed at James and staggered towards the shore. George grabbed his arm as he stumbled but he again shook himself free growling, "Get away white man." Then the fight seemed to leave him and he allowed himself to be led away quietly by Moses and Tallboy.

The moon returned to show the chastened figure of Leintu hurrying towards James who had thrown himself panting on the grass.

"You alright comrade?" he asked gruffly.

James rose slowly and glared at Leintu "Your inability to control your temper might be the death of us one of these days," he said quietly but with such force that Jenny shivered.

"You two need to get dry by the fire," she said and started half-running away from the lake.

Jenny smiled wryly when she saw Nelson, wrapped in a blanket, being tended to by Dr. Fatti.

People were standing around talking excitedly in small groups. Jenny noticed with relief that the children were still playing unconcernedly by Mrs. Mapilo's chair.

"You need to get those wet clothes off," said Pearl handing mugs of coffee to James and George.

"It's alright thank you ma'am," said James politely sipping the coffee and warming himself by the fire.

George stood slightly apart; droplets of water glistened in his blonde hair and his dripping clothes stuck to his body emphasising the contours of his lean but powerful frame. Jenny found herself looking at him in undisguised admiration.

George caught her gaze, smiled and said, "I need to get out of these wet things. Can I give you a lift home."

Jenny hoped that the confused emotions the question brought did not show on her face. Turning away slightly before she answered she saw David half asleep on Mrs. Mapilo's knee. Mr. Maplio had still not arrived.

For a wild moment Jenny thought of leaving the boys to be brought back by the Mapilos as arranged. While I do what? her conscience asked herself angrily.

Calmly she faced George. "Thank you very much. I think it's time David was home and it might be a while before Mr. Mapilo comes."

She walked across to where Sue and Larry were handing out food and drink anxiously trying to keep the party going.

"I think I'll slip away now if you don't mind," she said.

Larry clasped her hand, "Jenny you're a great dancer. Won't you stay longer?"

"No, thanks all the same. It's time I got the boys to bed." Mrs. Mapilo smiled understandingly as Jenny took David from her. George took Darren's hand. They quickly said goodbye, climbed into the truck and drove away.

Chapter Nine

For the next two weeks Jenny lived in a strange fantasy world. Images of George were with her almost constantly except when she found herself reliving her ecstatic dance with James. Her dreams were troubled and she would sometimes feel James's melancholy presence as she lay in the twilight world between waking and sleep. One night she awoke in horror from a dream in which James dived into the dam to save Leintu but hit his head against a rock and never re-surfaced. In the moonlight she could see ripples on the water where he had gone under, the circle of ripples became larger and larger until the water surged towards the shore where Jenny was standing and threatened to pull her down too. As Jenny lay staring into the darkness trying to shake off the horror of the dream she was at first calmed then irritated by Richard's regular breathing beside her. Once again she found her thoughts drifting back to George and once again she relived every detail of the journey back from the dam after the eventful party.

The boys had slept and Jenny had felt totally relaxed sitting in the dark cab beside the man who, only four days previously, had been a stranger. Neither of them had felt inclined to talk about what had happened at the party. They asked each other a lot of questions, each trying to get to know the other better. It was only as they neared the hospital that George referred to the family's proposed trip across the Vandu to Fort Joan. Jenny said that she expected a letter from Pam any day giving her arrival date and George again said that he would call in a couple of weeks on his way to Munari.

She was relieved to find Richard was not in when they arrived. George helped her carry the children to the house, looked ruefully down at his wet footsteps on the verandah, and was gone.

Jenny waited guiltily for Richard to comment on her preoccupation but he seemed increasingly unaware of her. Sometimes she felt they were like actors in a play; they said their lines effortlessly but their feelings were with the real world off-stage. Jenny smiled to herself when she thought of the analogy; it might be true that Richard's real world was outside the house in the hospital wards and operating theatre but for her the real world was the government house and garden with routine trips into the small town somewhere in the middle of Africa. Despite that, her fantasy world, focussing increasingly on the farm at the foot of the Vandu mountains, was becoming more real to her as each day merged into the next.

Darren and David, sensing their mother's preoccupation, spent as much time as possible out of the house. They played with Joshua most afternoons and in the mornings they were often to be found at the Fatti's house. Despite her flamboyant appearance Mrs. Fatti was a homely woman. She missed her two children who were at boarding school and was delighted to have Darren and David's company. She genuinely enjoyed having them in the kitchen helping her pound spices in the preparation of exotic dishes. She had endless patience and showed them how to make mouth-watering sweets and biscuits.

Jenny made little effort to pull herself out of her trance-like state, telling herself that in just a few weeks Pam would be with her. She felt that she could contain her varied emotions towards Richard, George and James until her friend came. In her mind she recounted the evening of the party as she would tell it to Pam. They would giggle and speculate as they had done in the old days when they had shared a flat together. She knew that Pam's company would inject her with the vitality she needed.

It had been Pam who, twelve years previously, had been such a support to her when her father had been killed in a car crash. It had been a sad grey time living with her father's unmarried sister for the last six months of her school career. Not surprisingly she had done badly in her exams, her aunt was finding her presence irksome and she did not know what to do. It was Pam who suggested that they enrol for a course on computer programming and share a flat together in London. Gradually Jenny's confidence had returned and she began to enjoy life anew but since then she had always regarded Pam as a life-line. Each afternoon when Richard came home Jenny would look impatiently to see if he was carrying a letter from her friend. She was beginning to get anxious that she had not heard from her for two months. And she wanted to know exactly when she was coming so that she could tell George when he next came to Bambo.

"There's no need to put the clothes away thank you Isaac. I can do it myself," Jenny tried to speak civilly to the elderly servant as he came into her bedroom with a pile of perfectly ironed clothes. She had told him several times that there was no need to iron the underwear but he insisted that he had done it that way for Mrs. Ferguson. She managed to stop him from putting the clothes away in the drawers but recently she had been so preoccupied that she had not bothered to do the job herself. "Yes madam," replied Isaac inscrutably avoiding looking at the pile of yesterday's laundry on the chair. He left the room soundlessly, stooping to pick up a coffee cup from beside the bed on his way. Jenny sighed in exasperation. Her feeling towards Isaac had always been ambivalent. On the one hand it was a great help having someone to do the housework in the heat but on the other she felt his presence an intrusion on her privacy.
Mechanically she picked up Richard's crisply starched white coat and put it on a hanger.
"Mummy, what can we do, Joshua's stayed at school this afternoon," shouted Darren running into the bedroom.

"Oh I don't know. Can't you amuse yourselves," snapped Jenny.

"We want to go to town," said David climbing on to the bed.

"Get off the bed with those filthy feet," yelled Jenny.

David sat on the bed looking at his feet in bewilderment.

"Take us to town Mummy," wheedled Darren.

"There's nothing to do in town," said Jenny sharply.

"We can go to the trains," said David.

Jenny's heart lurched. "We went to the trains last week," she frowned. Or was it the week before? she asked herself. Silently she started counting. It was Monday today. She had met George at the station on a Wednesday, the day after her birthday nearly three weeks ago. Was it as long as that? He should be back any day now.

"Can we Mummy?" David's voice jerked her back to reality.

"No, not today." Jenny looked at Richard's sock in her hand and found she had screwed it into a tight ball.

"But there's nothing to do here," Darren's voice penetrated Jenny's thoughts.

"No there isn't. Okay we'll go to town, I need some eggs. We'll see if we can get some from Mr. Farouk." Jenny suddenly sprang into action and shoved the rest of the clothes into a drawer. "Go and put on your shoes while I get the car keys."

When Jenny first came to Bambo she had bought eggs from the market but, as well as being small, they were often bad. Later she found that Mr. Farouk, one of the Indian traders, sold fresh eggs from chickens that he kept himself.

"Can we go and see Larry and Sue afterwards?" asked Darren as they got into the car.

"No not this week, they're too busy with exams."

"What's exams?" asked David.

"Ask your father," replied Jenny irritably.

"But Daddy's at work."

"Quiet while I'm driving," said Jenny. She gave a scream and slammed on the brakes as a child ran in front of the car. It came to a halt just in front of the terrified child. Crouching on the road was a little girl about two years old, naked except for a string of beads around her waist. Shaking, Jenny got out of the car, picked up the child and strode to the side of the road.

"Whose child is this?" she demanded to the small crowd that was already gathering. A spindly, poorly dressed girl of eight or nine held out her arms and whispered in Chakari, "She's my sister." Gently Jenny handed her the child. "Where is your mother?" she asked in Chakari. She was not able to follow the torrent that followed but gathered that the mother was farming somewhere out of town. The bodies of the crowd pressed around her as they added their opinions and admonished the girl. "Okay, well, look after her better in future," said Jenny as she pushed past the excited onlookers and got back into the car.

Jenny was still shaking when she parked under a tree opposite Farouk's store. As she was locking the doors she was accosted by a large woman generously doused with cheap perfume. She was very black and dressed in a traditional cotton wrapper and blouse.

"Ah, Mrs. North, how are you?"

"I'm fine. How are you?" replied Jenny politely trying desperately to remember where she had seen the woman before.

"I am quite better now thanks to your husband. I suffered such pains in my abdomen. How I suffered. I went to the witchdoctor but he just took my money. Then I heard about the new white doctor in town. So I made an appointment to see him. As a private patient you understand. He gave me medicine and said "Mrs. Denu, take this for a while and if that fails we will have to operate.""

Jenny smiled mechanically, her mind still on the naked child in the road. She remembered the woman now, Mrs. Denu the wife of one of the richer market traders. She had Richard at her beck and call the whole week she had been in hospital. Jenny made an effort to concentrate on what the woman was saying ".......such a wonderful doctor. So devoted. And how the nurses love him. They will do anything for Doctor North. Please greet him for me. Tell him I am as fit as a fiddle now thanks to his good doctoring."

"Oh yes, I'll tell him. Goodbye," said Jenny propelling the boys towards the store.

"So devoted. How the nurses love him." Mrs. Denu's words rang in Jenny's ears as she walked across the road. Jenny tried to remind herself that people had enthused about Richard before. Previously she had been proud that he was so highly regarded but now she was just angry and suspicious.

The store was cool and dark compared with the heat and glare outside and Jenny managed to calm down enough to greet Mr. Farouk politely and ask for some eggs. There were just six left.

"They are very fresh madam," the Indian assured her as he carefully put the large brown eggs in a paper bag.

"They look lovely. We'll have boiled eggs for tea."
Looking at them Jenny was suddenly transported back to her childhood when she used to go with her parents to stay at her uncle's farm in Wiltshire. She used to help her aunt collect the eggs and afterwards she was allowed to select hers for tea.

"I want to carry them," said Darren tugging at her arm.
"No you might drop them."
"No I won't," insisted Darren.

Once again Jenny saw herself as a little girl helping her aunt carry in the eggs.

"Alright," she said reluctantly handing him the bag.

They left the shop and started to cross the road back to the car.

"Look, there's a monkey!" cried David pointing to a man with a monkey on his shoulder.

"Where? Oh yes. See the monkey!" shouted Darren running towards it.

"Mind the eggs!" yelled Jenny. But it was too late. Darren had tripped over a stone and the bag fell to the ground. The sticky yellow liquid started to seep through the paper on to the sand.

"You naughty, naughty boy!" shrieked Jenny grabbing Darren by the shoulders and shaking him. "I told you to be careful," and she raised her hand to strike him.

"No madam!" cried an old man who had been standing watching. "The child does not know what he does."

Jenny glared at him speechless with anger at Darren and with shame at herself for making a scene in public.

At that moment a thin ragged-looking brown dog limped up to the bag and sniffed. Its drooping tail began to wag and it gave a few excited yelps before gulping down the broken eggs, paper bag and all.

"See, someone is satisfied," said the man, his lined face creased into a smile.

Jenny however was in no mood for philosophising.

"Come boys," she said grabbing their hands and pushing them into the car.

When they got back Isaac was waiting in the kitchen.

"Mr. Farrier come to see you madam," he said smiling.

"Where is he?" cried Jenny feeling her face flush a fiery red. "Is he here?" She looked eagerly around.

"He says he is at the rest house. He will go to Munari tomorrow."

"Oh. Thank you Isaac. Has the doctor come back yet?" she added.

"No madam."

"Okay." Jenny brushed her hand distractedly through her hair. "Well I'll see you tomorrow."

"Yes madam. Goodbye." Isaac looked at her keenly and was gone.

"Can we go and see if Joshua's home?" asked Darren.

"Yes, run along," said Jenny anxious to be alone.

She quickly had a shower and changed then got herself a cold drink and sat down on the verandah trying to compose her thoughts. She and Richard still hadn't discussed the trip to Fort Joan. She had been putting off bringing up the subject until she heard from Pam.

She looked at her watch. It was four o'clock. Richard could be back any time now. She wondered what sort of day he had had. She remembered the child running in front of the car and shivered.

"Hello," said Richard opening the gate. "You look like a lady of leisure sitting there.

Jenny scowled and was about to say something when she noticed the letter in his hand.

"Who's that from?" she shrilled.

"It's addressed to you; looks like Pam's writing," said Richard handing her the letter as he walked into the house. Jenny ripped open the envelope and took out a sheet of paper. It's shorter than usual, she thought as she started to read it.

Flat 2A,
Orchard Court,
London. S.E. 15.
May, 5th.
Dear Jenny,
I'm sorry I've been so long in writing and I hope this won't come as too much of a shock

*to you. I didn't write earlier because I was
still hoping that I would be able to come to
Chark as planned. I'm really disappointed
that I won't be able to see you but - now
wait for it - by the time you get this letter
I'll be married! I mentioned Ian in my last
letter and I believe I told you that he works
for an oil company. Well he has suddenly
been posted to Jakarta. We hadn't any plans
to get married but when he told me he would
be away for two years we both suddenly
realised that we didn't want to be apart.
And as the only way we could stay together
was to get married we decided we had better
get on with it. There's even a good
possibility of me getting a job when we get
there. But at the moment I'm not worried
about that, it might be rather nice to be a
lady of leisure for a while. The prospect of
going to the Far East is really exciting. Do
you remember how we used to say we'd go round
the world together? Perhaps you could go
home via Indonesia. It would be super to see
you. I'm only sorry it can't be next month
as planned. I hope it doesn't upset your
plans too much. I'll write and tell you all
about it when we get there.
Regards to Richard, love to the boys, and to
yourself,*

Pam.

Jenny looked disbelievingly at the paper in her hand. Pam
married? Surely not. And to someone she hadn't even
met. What was he like? Jenny looked at the letter again.
"I'm only sorry it can't be next month as planned. I hope it
doesn't upset your plans too much." The words leapt out at

Jenny until her eyes filled with tears and they disappeared into a nonsensical blur.

"When's she coming?" asked Richard as he came out with a glass in his hand.

Silently Jenny handed him the letter.

"So the gay girl's getting married. Don't envy the fellow," said Richard handing the letter back when he'd read it.

Jenny stared at him angrily.

"It's disappointing for you though," he said quickly.

"Yes," said Jenny flatly. Then added, "And it's spoilt our holiday."

"Holiday?"

"We were going to go up to Mutape and then across to the mountains. And then we were invited to go and stay with George Farrier on the other side of the Vandu near Fort Joan. To make it a round trip," gulped Jenny as she saw the look of incomprehension on Richard's face.

"Yes. Well I suppose there's no point now."

"But we might as well go anyway. After all, you've applied for the leave."

Richard looked embarrassed.

"You have applied for leave haven't you?" demanded Jenny suspiciously.

"Well, yes I believe I mentioned I'd be taking a week in June. But I couldn't apply for it officially until we knew exactly when Pam was coming," said Richard defensively.

"I don't believe you want to go."

"Well..........it's just that it's not a very good time. Dr. Fatti doesn't seem to be settling in very well. He's upsetting some of the nurses and I'm trying to smooth things over."

"But you're overworking. You need a holiday," said Jenny desperately.

"But I'm needed Jenny."

Jenny got up. "Well, I need to get out for a little while. The boys are with Joshua. You're not on call are you?" Richard shook his head. "Where are you going?"

"I might pop over and see Sue and Larry. See you later."
Jenny drove the Beetle carefully through town. She went
straight on at the turn off to the secondary school and took
the road out of town. Before it reached the main road she
took a right-hand turn and wound slowly up the hill to the
rest house.

Chapter Ten

"Hello Jenny. So you got my message. It's good to see you." George flung open the door of the hut in response to Jenny's hesitant knock. "Shall we go across and have a drink?" he asked as Jenny stood in the doorway.

"No thanks. I won't stay long. I just came to say......" Jenny felt suddenly dizzy and leant against the door for support. "I've just had a bit of a shock," she said.

George looked at her with concern. "Come and sit down," he said gently shutting the door behind him.

Jenny sat on the edge of the bed and breathed deeply. She looked at George, his tanned muscular body framed by the door. "What's happened?" he prompted.

"It's Pam. She's not coming." To her dismay Jenny burst into tears.

George sat down beside her and put his arm round her. "I'm so sorry, that must be a real disappointment."

"Yes," Jenny sniffed, "and it's not just that. It's............"

"Yes?"

Jenny hesitated. She felt the comfort of George's body and put her head on his shoulder.

George drew in a breath and held her closer. "What else is the matter?"

"Well," Jenny whispered. "Now we won't be going to the Vandu and so we won't be coming to stay with you."

"Oh Jenny. Do you really care that much?"

Jenny looked at him and smiled. "Yes."

For a moment they just sat quietly looking at each other. Jenny felt the tension of the last three weeks evaporate. Instead of guiltily asking herself what she was doing there Jenny felt a strange sense of peace. She looked at George half-expectantly her face a mixture of tranquillity and vitality. There was an urgency in George's eyes as he met her gaze and tentatively kissed her. When he felt her respond he laid her gently back on the bed.

Time seemed to stand still. The uncertainties and frustrations that Jenny had suffered vanished as she abandoned herself to the present. There was no worry that the telephone might ring or the children call, no disillusionment that the act was just a mechanical matrimonial rite. Instead the time that followed was one of joy and excitement as she discovered, as if for the first time, the delights of her body and found it in harmony with the man beside her.

Gradually, the ecstasy diminished and they lay quietly together feeling the heartbeat of the other slowly return to normal. Jenny looked up at the golden thatch of the conical roof. The dark poles came to a point in the centre and were bound together by straw-coloured twine. The straw gave out a pungent smell that fleetingly reminded her of late summer days spent on the farm with her parents when she was a child.

"Tell me more about Rossano," she said wistfully.

"Jenny, you must come and see it for yourself," said George urgently.

She shrugged. "I don't think that's possible now."

"But I thought you had planned to take leave next month anyway. You can still come."

"What all of us?" Jenny sounded slightly incredulous. "And anyway," she added, "Richard never did apply for leave. He never wanted to go. He couldn't bear the thought of being away from the hospital." She spoke flatly trying to keep the bitterness out of her voice.

George gently stroked her hair. "Well, I think you could do with a holiday. Why don't you come?"

Jenny's eyes sparkled at the thought, but she said quickly, "Oh no, I couldn't leave the boys."

"Bring them too," said George persuasively.

Jenny said nothing. She kissed George lightly on the nose, swung herself out of bed and said, "Talking of the boys, I think I should be getting back now."

George put out his hand as if to restrain her then thought better of it. "Well, think about it. I'll be back here about this time on Thursday. Will you meet me here then?"
Pulling her dress over her head Jenny thought in panic, "What am I letting myself in for?" Then she looked at George, his tanned face glowing and his eyes soft as he looked at her. "Do you want me to?" she asked as lightly as she could.
"Jenny, you know I do," he said getting up and kissing her. She could feel the excitement in his naked body as he held her close and she responded with passion.
"Stay a little longer," he whispered.
Jenny glanced towards the window. The sun had just set and the sky was streaked with crimson and gold.
Gently she pushed him away. "I must get back," she said. George nodded and quickly dressed.
He opened the door and they stood for a moment in the doorway looking at the darkening sky. A bat swooped towards them then away again.
"Twilight is such a special time in Africa," reflected Jenny. "It's so beautiful and yet over so quickly."
"Yes," said George seriously looking down at her.
Jenny shivered slightly despite the warmth of his arm around her. Perhaps that's how it's going to be with us, she thought. Night follows quickly on twilight in this part of the world.
Jenny gave him a quick kiss. "Don't come with me, I'll see myself to the car. Drive safely to Munari. I'll see you when you get back on Thursday."
"Goodbye Jenny. Take care." George stood silently watching long after she had walked to the Beetle and driven away.

. . . .

Richard was working at his desk when Jenny got home. He looked up and smiled as she walked in.

"Hello. Are you feeling a bit better?"

"Oh. Yes." Jenny was disconcerted by his interest. "Are the boys back yet?"

"No." Richard looked out of the window. "Oh, it's almost dark, I wondered why I couldn't see very well. Shall we walk along and fetch them?"

Jenny looked surprised, they weren't in the habit of calling on Matron. "Okay."

"We won't stop, I just thought it would be nice to have a stroll."

"Okay," said Jenny again.

"I think this is my favourite time of the day," said Richard as they walked past the ivory coloured frangipani tree perfuming the air around it with its heady fragrance.

"Yes. It's lovely." Jenny could not think of anything else to say. Richard was walking quickly and she had to almost run to keep up with him. "What's the hurry?" she asked with forced gaiety.

"Hurry?" Richard frowned then laughed self-consciously. "It's habit I suppose." He made a visible effort to slow his pace. "Sometimes the nurses call me Dr. Hurry," he said half confidingly.

"What did they call you at home?" Jenny felt as if she was making polite conversation with a stranger.

"Oh they didn't bother to find names for small fry like me."

Jenny could hear the bitterness in his voice and noticed that his fists were clenched. Part of her wanted to hold him and say that it was all over now, that he had proved that he could hold his own as a doctor even under difficult circumstances. But she could not.

They reached Matron's house and found Darren and David playing with Joshua in the garden. Matron came out when she heard them arrive. She was still wearing her uniform and, even without the imperious lace cap, she looked formidable.

"Will you take tea?" It was more of a command than a request.

"Thank you Matron," Richard flung an apologetic look at Jenny.

Matron summoned Joshua to put three dining chairs on the verandah, then bustled inside to organise the tea.

"The girl will bring tea soon," said Matron coming out again and settling her stout body on the hard chair.

Jenny smiled nervously and felt angry with herself that she always felt reduced to a silly schoolgirl in Matron's presence.

"Those are pretty," she prattled pointing to a clump of pink lazyman flowers growing by the path.

"Oh, my garden isn't nearly as good as yours," said Matron complacently. "But then Mrs. Ferguson took so much trouble with the garden. She had green hands."

"Jenny works hard in our garden," said Richard.

"Dr. Ferguson found the garden so relaxing to come home to after a busy day at the hospital," continued Matron as if she had not heard. "Ah, here's the tea. Put it there Sissie," she said indicating a wooden stool.

Matron had just handed out the delicate china cups when a nurse opened the gate. She greeted Matron respectfully in Chakari then turned to Richard.

"Sister Ningi says please can you go and help in casualty."

"But Dr. Fatti's on duty this evening."

"He's there, but she asked me to send for you as well."

Richard pursed his lips and looked nervously at Jenny.

"Very well. Please excuse me Matron." He drank his tea quickly. "See you later Jenny." He got up and followed the nurse out of the gate.

"Thank you for the tea Matron," said Jenny as soon as she had finished her cup.

"You're welcome. Mrs. Ferguson and I often used to have a cup together in the evening."

Jenny said nothing but felt a vague sense of envy. It must have been nice for Mrs. Ferguson to have a neighbour of a similar age and with whom she had interests in common. Jenny knew that if she attended church she would have more friends and acquaintances in town but it would be hypocritical to go for that reason.

She called her children, bid Matron and Joshua goodnight and walked home. As she prepared their supper she talked gaily to the boys and determinedly banished thoughts of George from her mind though every now and again an image of Richard in close consultation with Sister Ningi flashed in front of her.

The boys were in bed and Jenny was sitting in the lounge with a newspaper on her lap when Richard arrived back from the hospital. His brow was furrowed and his eyes blinked anxiously behind his spectacles.

"Trouble?" asked Jenny making a determined effort to be sympathetic.

"No. But it was tricky." Richard took off his glasses and wiped his eyes with a clean handkerchief. "Dr. Fatti wasn't too happy when he saw me but I think Sister Ningi was right to call me."

"What was the problem?" Jenny's tone must have conveyed her lack of interest for Richard simply shrugged and said, " I'll get some coffee."

Jenny felt annoyed with them both that she was unable to reach out to Richard. She reminded herself that she had tried often enough in the last eighteen months. And now it was too late. She had committed herself to another man now.

"But that's silly," argued her other voice. "Just because you've slept with somebody once doesn't commit you to them. Lots to people do it all the time. Maybe George does," the voice taunted her. "Maybe he's got another woman in Munari and one in Fort Joan too." Jenny sat gazing unseeing at the familiar objects around her. Instead she saw the expression in George's eyes as he begged her to stay and almost felt his solid comforting presence beside her and she knew intuitively that this was something special for him too.

"I think I'll take my coffee to bed."

Jenny started as Richard broke in on her thoughts. She nodded mutely and tried to smile at him. She was unaware of the subtle change in her, her skin glowed and she had an aura of suppressed excitement about her. She was unaware of the sudden expression of longing on Richard's face as he looked at her. Unaware of their mutual loss. Richard hovered in the doorway holding the coffee cup.

"I'll read for a little while. Coming?" he said hesitantly.

"Not yet. I'm not tired," replied Jenny shutting him out.

. . . .

The boys got on Jenny's nerves more than usual the next day. They seemed to sense the strangeness in the air and reacted against it.

Jenny felt Isaac's reproachful stare as she screamed at David for spilling a glass of water. She had an uncanny feeling that the African could read her thoughts and she felt suddenly unclean. The increasing humidity drained her energy and she sat listlessly waiting for the day to pass. And the next. Waiting for George's return.

"It shouldn't be as hot as this in May," complained Jenny at lunch time.

"It seems like a big storm brewing up somewhere," answered Richard. He looked at her keenly. "You look tired. Why don't you have a rest this afternoon."

"I'm alright," replied Jenny shortly.

Nevertheless, after Richard had gone she asked Isaac to keep an eye on the boys and went to her bedroom. She did not think she was tired but the oppressiveness of the atmosphere overcame her and she fell into a deep sleep.

She was awakened about an hour later by a terrifying bellow. She leapt out of bed and rushed to the window fearing that someone was being attacked. The noise was primeval, not quite human yet its pitch was heart-searing. Everything looked the same outside but, now that she was thoroughly awake, Jenny slipped on her sandals and went out on to the verandah.

A donkey was shambling along the path towards the garden gate.

She smiled in relief. Donkeys were a rare sight in the hospital compound but she remembered that soon after their arrival they had been wakened by a donkey's frantic braying. She closed the gate behind the donkey then wandered round the back of the house.

"Oh no!" she screamed. The water melon patch had been completely trampled. The remnants of the squashy pink flesh of half a dozen ripening water melons was mixed with earth. Already the bloated sugar ants had moved in to make their picking.

Jenny bent down to see if there was anything she could salvage. Then she quickly recoiled in horror as she saw the sockets of a small skull looking up at her. A mass of small bones and a few tattered feathers lay scattered around.

"Oh my God, it dug up the owl," whispered Jenny as she turned away trying to shake off the feeling of foreboding that threatened to overwhelm her.

. . . .

There was no rain but the oppressiveness continued the following day. Jenny wandered about aimlessly as Isaac industriously removed all the furniture and vigorously polished the floors. She avoided the boys as much as possible, she couldn't face Isaac's look of reproach if she shouted at them and she knew it would take very little to provoke her.

At one point David came running in with a grazed knee and mechanically Jenny bathed it and put a plaster on. She dried his tears and gave him a biscuit but neglected to ask how he had done it because her thoughts were elsewhere. She was sitting in the lounge gazing idly at the brightly polished floor when she heard Darren scream. It took a moment before it penetrated her thoughts that she had to do something about it. By the time she got outside Isaac was already carrying Darren towards the house, blood streaming from his forehead.

David trotted breathlessly up to his mother. "He fell out of the tree house," he said pointing to a plank of wood balancing precariously on a branch of the jacaranda tree. "Quickly Isaac, go and get Dr. North," said Jenny taking the sobbing child from the old man.

She went inside and lay Darren down on the settee then took a clean handkerchief to staunch the gaping wound. She looked up with relief when Richard walked in.

"It's a jagged cut. How did you do it son?" he asked tenderly as he examined the white-faced child.

"There was a nail in the wood," volunteered David importantly.

"What the hell were you letting them play with that for?" Richard glared at Jenny. "He'll need a couple of stitches and a tetanus shot. Come Darren, we'll go now. How could you be so irresponsible Jenny," said Richard as he hurriedly left the house with Darren over his shoulder.

Jenny sat stunned by the accusation. Her head whirled as she thought of all the times she had played with them, had fed and dressed them and kept them out of danger.

"Well I'm finished with the lot of them," she muttered angrily to herself.

"What Mummy?" asked David.

"Oh nothing. Shall we go and see Mrs. Fatti?"

"Oh yes. She makes nice cookies."

Jenny was disappointed to see the car port was empty as they approached the Fatti's house. They knocked to make sure but no-one was in.

Slowly they trailed back along the road through their gate. The carefully tended garden and shady trees failed to bring the sense of relaxation that they normally did. Instead Jenny's eyes went straight to the water melon patch and to the peeling paint on the walls of the house.

"I can't take it any longer," she muttered desperately. "I can't be stuck here for another year or maybe more with no-one to talk to."

"I'm thirsty Mummy," said David plaintively.

Wearily Jenny took his hand and they went to the kitchen. She took the tin of powdered milk and made up a jug of milk with cold water from the fridge. David was satisfied but Jenny felt she would give anything to walk outside and find a bottle of fresh milk on the doorstep.

She put the kettle on and waited listlessly for Richard and Darren to return.

Darren was full of self-importance when they came back and was eager to tell his brother about the treatment he received especially as it was the beautiful Sister Ningi who had helped his father stitch him up.

As Jenny listened she felt suddenly defeated. All at once her six years of motherhood, her marriage to Richard, her position as a computer programmer dissolved into nothing. Now that her friend was no longer coming her link with reality as she understood it was gone. In a flash of intuition she realised that the link for Richard had been broken long ago; it had started with his family's hostility during Bill's accident and had finally snapped their first Christmas in Chark when his mother had not even bothered to write. For Richard reality now was the hospital in Bambo. Jenny realised that like Dr. Ferguson, Richard would be content to devote himself to the hospital

for years. But it was different for her, she was no
missionary's wife. What was going to happen to her?
Richard drank his coffee quickly, patted Darren on the
head and said, "I'll be getting back now."
Jenny raised her eyebrows questioningly.
"I'm on duty this evening but I finish at 4.30 tomorrow
then I'm off for the whole week-end."
"What, even Friday?"
"Yes. Unless of course anything serious happens."
Richard laughed half-apologetically.
Jenny nodded absently as Richard walked out of the door.
She stared at his back hurrying down the path as if she had
never seen him before. A whole week-end off? What
would they do? What would they say to each other?
Mechanically Jenny gave the boys their supper, bathed
them, read them a story and put them to bed.
She felt light-headed as she sat on the verandah gazing
into the darkness and waiting for Richard to come home.
She knew that they should talk to each other before it was
too late. But she did not know what to say. Should she
tell him about George? Make accusations about Sister
Ningi? No, they weren't the root of the problem. What
was the problem then? That Richard took her for granted?
That he was fulfilled and she wasn't? Or was it the
accumulated loneliness of being an expatriate wife and
mother in a small town in the middle of Africa? Certainly
her life was busy enough in providing the boys with a little
of what they were missing at home. But her craving for
company on a footing different from that of the doctor's
wife was beginning to overwhelm her. Jenny wrung her
hands silently in the darkness and wondered whether she
would feel differently if her parents were still alive. She
suddenly felt an unbearable loneliness take hold of her and
she held her head in her hands in despair.
She was aroused by Richard's footsteps and looked up
expectantly. As he opened the gate Jenny took a breath

and prepared herself to make an opening that would start them talking about their situation. She knew it wasn't going to be easy for she could sense that Richard was still angry with her for Darren's accident.

"Richard," she said then stopped in fright as she heard a low hoot.

"What's that?" she asked querulously.

"It's just an owl," said Richard irritably walking past her and going into the house.

Jenny knew then that she had lost .

"In Africa, owls are supposed to be portents of evil," she murmured but Richard was already in the kitchen busily making himself a cup of coffee and a sandwich.

"Can I get you anything?" asked Jenny following him into the kitchen.

"It's alright thank you. How's Darren?"

"He's okay. They went to bed without any trouble this evening."

Richard nodded and carried his supper to the dining room.

"I've been thinking about our holiday," said Jenny hesitantly as she sat down in the chair opposite Richard.

"What holiday?"

"Our holiday to the Vandu."

"I thought we discussed that before. I told you I'm too busy to take leave now."

"And what about me?" Jenny said timorously.

"You?"

"Yes." Jenny could feel her voice trembling.

"You can do what you like." Richard yawned. "I'm awfully tired, I've had a busy day. I'll have a bath and go to bed."

Richard got up and left the room leaving his cup and plate on the table.

Jenny sat for a long while staring unseeing at the blank white wall in front of her. She hadn't said the things she had wanted to. The owl had unnerved her.

"You can do what you like." Richard had said.
Well perhaps she would.

. . . .

By four o'clock the following day Jenny was in a state of
utter turmoil. Her desire to be with George again was
overwhelming but, as the time drew nearer, she was
plagued with doubts. Had he meant what he said? Would
he even be there? And what about his invitation to
Rossano? Since her inability to communicate with
Richard the night before she was losing her last grip on
reality and was beginning to regard the thought of leaving
her husband and children to travel to the other side of
Chark with a man she hardly knew as the most normal
thing in the world.
As soon as she heard Richard's footsteps on the path Jenny
picked up the car keys and walked out of the house.
"I'm just popping out to town," she said.
"Oh. Alright. Will you be long?" asked Richard looking
puzzled and slightly hurt.
Jenny pretended not to hear but gave him a radiant smile
as she reached the car and drove off.
When she turned into the rest house and saw the old
Bedford parked beside the thatched hut Jenny was almost
paralysed with fear and excitement. The engine stalled
and she revved it loudly as she tried to start it, still
wondering whether to turn round and go home or park in
the car park and walk brazenly over to George's door.
A car hooted impatiently behind her and Jenny shot
forward and came to a halt under the bougainvillea. She
shot a nervous glance at the driver of the other car
wondering if it was anyone she knew. The Charkian
nodded politely to her as he got out and walked across to
the rest house. Slowly Jenny got out of the beetle and
wound up the windows. She was so absorbed in her
thoughts that she did not hear footsteps coming towards

her. She looked up as a shadow fell across the car and George was standing in front of her. Instinctively they held out their hands to each other, their faces illuminated as they looked into the other's eyes and saw mirrored in them their own desire. They laughed in delight, looked around to see if they were being observed and laughed again.

"Did you have a good journey?" asked Jenny as matter-of-factly as she could.

"Yes thank you. And you - how have you been since - Monday?" George looked at her with love and concern.

"Monday?" sparkled Jenny. "It seems like only yesterday or even this morning. But tell me about your trip to Munari."

George looked at her quizzically. "Would you like a drink?" he asked.

Jenny felt suddenly parched. "Yes please."

They walked across to the rest house, bought two beers then came out again.

George hesitated at one of the tables. "Would you like to sit here?" he asked politely, "or," he looked at her questioningly, his eyes soft and sparkling, "shall we go to my room?"

At that moment the Charkian came out and walked noiselessly over to collect something from his car.

"It'll be quieter in your room," said Jenny seriously.

George made a funny face and looked at the empty tables and the silent Charkian and they both laughed.

The sun went behind a cloud but to Jenny everything seemed bathed in a radiant light as she walked with George to the thatched hut.

The urgency that they had felt on the previous occasion now gave way to a carefree laughter. They sat, sipping their beer and chatting inconsequentially before they abandoned themselves to a love-making that seemed sweeter and more intense than Jenny could ever remember.

Gradually the shadows lengthened, the sun went down and they lay quietly together, their bodies touching, neither wishing to make the first move. A move which would bring them crashing back to reality.

"Did you think any more about coming to Rossano?" asked George diffidently.

"I thought about it all the time," she replied simply.

"When are you coming?" Jenny felt the power in his body as he asked, almost demanded.

"When are you leaving?" returned Jenny.

"Tomorrow. At sun-rise. Will you come with me?" George looked at her in disbelief.

"Yes, I'll come," Jenny heard herself say.

"Your husband.........?" George did not finish the sentence, not wishing to say more, fearing to lose her if he asked questions.

"I'll tell him I'm going."

She added to herself, justifying her decision, "I'm an irresponsible mother and an unfaithful wife. They'll be better off without me."

She did not see the look of inexpressible pain that crossed George's face as she spoke. He squeezed Jenny's hand tightly then let it go saying seriously, "Alright, my love, I'll meet you outside the hospital gates at five o'clock.

. . . .

As Jenny drove down the hill in the twilight she felt exhilarated. After being taken for granted by her husband and children for so long George's proposition was irresistible. She almost laughed aloud as she clutched the steering wheel and headed back towards the town. The unreality in which she had been living for the last few months had overtaken her completely. Her boys, who had previously occupied almost every waking moment, were no longer relevant as she mentally checked the things that she needed to take with her.

"Toothpaste," she murmured to herself and turned down the road to Farouk's store.

She parked the car and walked confidently into the shop, her head held high and an unconscious smile hovering round her lips.

"Good evening Mr. Farouk," she said gaily, her eyes darting among the shelves. She selected her toilet requisites and was just about to pay when she noticed several packets of digestive biscuits. They were Richard's favourite and rarely obtainable in Bambo.

"And two of those please," she added pointing to the biscuits. Richard will be pleased, she thought; it might cheer him up, he's been getting very tired lately, too involved with his work.

"Is that alright?" Mr Farouk looked at Jenny anxiously, puzzled by her change in mood.

"Oh. Yes, thank you." Jenny realised she had been frowning.

She put the biscuits at the bottom of her bag then gave a secret smile as she added the other things and caught a waft of perfumed soap.

I hadn't realised the doctor's wife was such an attractive woman thought Mr. Farouk as Jenny handed him the money then turned and left the shop, unconsciously swaying her hips as she went.

. . . .

Larry and Sue's motor bike was parked outside the house when Jenny arrived back.

"Where've you been Jenny?" asked Sue gaily as Jenny walked into the house.

"I've been visiting Mrs. Ntoo." Jenny was surprised how smoothly the lie came out. "How are the exams going?"

"We're fed up with marking," said Larry, "so we came to see how you folks were."

"Oh we're fine," beamed Jenny. "Will you have some supper with us?"

"Oh no, that's alright," said Sue.

"Do stay," urged Richard, "we haven't seen you in a long time. I didn't even see much of you at the party. I'm sorry I left early. I hope you weren't offended," he added awkwardly.

Jenny stared in amazement, unwilling to believe her ears. "Oh don't worry about that," said Sue easily. "But if you're sure it's no trouble it would be nice to stay, wouldn't it Larry?"

"Sure," agreed Larry busy with the lego model he was making amid eager instructions from Darren and David. Richard followed Jenny to the kitchen. "Is there anything I can do?" he asked.

Jenny felt confused. Richard had got out of the habit of helping in the kitchen and anyway she wanted to be alone. "Just keep them supplied with drinks and enjoy their company," she said.

Jenny said little throughout the evening but she had an aura of vitality and intrigue that infected the others. The tenseness left Richard's mouth as he regaled the American couple with their stories of his medical school days.

Unnoticed, Jenny went quietly to the bedroom and put a few things into her rucksack ready for the morning. The sight of it stirred her imagination. For years now the old rucksack had lain covered in dust but tomorrow she would be off again venturing forth to a new life.

"Remember the time we gate-crashed old Doc Murphy's party?" said Richard, his face animated as Jenny walked back into the room.

Jenny smiled and Richard recounted the tale. But Jenny would not let herself remember. That time was over now. She folded her hands in her lap and sat serenely waiting for her friends to go. Waiting for morning to come.

It was midnight before Larry and Sue left.

"That was a nice evening," said Richard as they made their way to bed.

"Yes," said Jenny. And thought: I'm glad I saw them before I left. She felt light-headed as she sat on the bed.

"Are you alright?" asked Richard.

"I think so," she replied vaguely. She was sure there was something she needed to tell him but she couldn't remember what it was.

Richard yawned as he got into bed. "It's a good thing I'm off tomorrow." He laughed unconcernedly. "I'm out of practice doing the morning rounds with a hangover."

Jenny smiled absently, her eyes large and shining. She switched off the light and snuggled under the bedcovers in a state of total relaxation.

Richard reached out for her hand, squeezed it gently and fell asleep.

Jenny gave a deep sigh, then she too was asleep.

Chapter Eleven

It was dark when Jenny woke up with a start. She felt
refreshed and fully awake. She looked at her watch. Half
past four. She would have to hurry.

Soundlessly she got up, not looking at Richard who was
sleeping deeply. A smile flickered across his face as he
subconsciously felt Jenny moving beside him. Without his
glasses he looked younger, vulnerable, almost childlike
with his arm flung behind his head. His features were
relaxed and his face glowed healthily. If Jenny had looked
she would have seen the face of the man she had married
ten years ago. But she did not look. Was aware only that
she had to get away from the stranger he had become.

She dressed quickly, took the rucksack from the cupboard
and crept along the passage to the kitchen. She filled the
kettle, then washed her face and cleaned her teeth while
the water boiled.

She took a sip of coffee trying to think what else it was she
had to do. She looked at her watch. A quarter to five.
She took another sip of coffee and then remembered what
it was. She hadn't told Richard she was going. She should
have told him last night. She brushed her hand through
her hair in agitation. Years of conditioning decided her,
she couldn't wake him, he needed his sleep.

Briskly, Jenny went to the desk and took out some writing
paper and a pen. With swift bold strokes she wrote:-

*Richard - you don't need me any more so I'm
going with George Farrier to his farm near
Fort Joan. I'm sure you'll understand.*

Jenny.

She paused, wondering whether to leave any messages for
the boys. The pen trembled in her hand. Decisively she

put it down, put the paper in an envelope, sealed it and wrote Richard's name with a flourish.

Jenny put the letter on the table and walked down the passage to take a last look at her sons. She could hear their regular breathing as she stopped outside their door. Instinct told her that if she went in now she would be lost. She looked at her watch again. Five minutes to five. George would be waiting for her in a few minutes, might even be there already. She turned and walked purposefully away, picked up her rucksack, quietly unlocked the door and let herself out of the house.

Standing for a moment on the verandah Jenny breathed in the fresh scents of a new day and felt the cool air on her bare arms. She almost laughed out loud as she looked up at the lightening sky and saw the morning star winking down at her. She swung the rucksack on her back and immediately felt a joyous sense of freedom. Briskly she strode down the path, through the gate and past the hospital buildings.

Jonah was slumped by the hospital gates, a dirty old raincoat pulled around him. He glowered suspiciously at her as she passed but even he could not dampen her spirits because ahead of her, discreetly parked under a large tree was George's truck.

As he saw her approaching George got out and came towards her his face shining in the half light. Jenny ran the last few paces and flung herself into his arms. Any qualms that she may have felt vanished as Jenny felt George's strong arms pulling her closer and the passion in his body as he kissed her. She wanted to make love there and then, she didn't care that they were still within Jonah's sullen gaze or that people would soon be leaving their compounds to get water from the standpipes or making an early start to the fields.

Moments, or hours, passed then George gently pulled away and said, "You look beautiful this morning."

Jenny flushed with pleasure and smiled, "It's a beautiful morning," she replied simply.

And indeed all the familiar sights seemed bathed in iridescence as they drove slowly through the town. As they crossed the bridge they saw a group of children digging in the soft sand for water to fill their buckets. The figures were silhouetted against the dawn sky and Jenny felt as if she was looking at a snap-shot that encapsulated the essence of Africa. An Africa of which she knew very little but which she was eager to discover now that she had left the confines of her family and her husband's hospital. They passed the turn-off to the secondary school, the railway station and the rest house turn off and came to a halt when they reached the main road. A donkey cart laden with firewood shambled along but apart from that the road was deserted. George put his foot down and Jenny laughed in delight as she felt the wind whistle through her hair.

George grinned and patted her knee. "Comfortable?" he asked and swerved slightly as he turned his head to look at Jenny.

"I'm fine," she said looking at him with sparkling eyes.

"I'm afraid it's not a very romantic method of transport," George laughed half apologetically.

"It's just right," said Jenny emphatically.

" I don't really like taking it to Munari but I was dropping off a couple of bulls along the way so I had to bring it. We'll slow down once we get on the dirt road."

To their right they could see golden streaks in the sky as the sun began to rise then they turned off the tar road and headed due west.

"This is the way to Amos's farm," said Jenny.

"It's the way to my farm too - in another five hundred kilometres." George kept his eyes on the road this time but they were both aware of the electric current of mutual attraction that passed between them.

The noise of the engine made conversation difficult and they continued for the next couple of hours absorbed in their thoughts. Jenny looked out of the window drinking in everything and giving an exclamation of delight as she noticed an unusual bird or flower, a distant hill or a cluster of huts and people going about their business. Once when George looked at Jenny pointing enthusiastically out of the window a shadow passed across his face and he closed his eyes momentarily as if trying to shut off some half-forgotten pain. Then he leant across and put his hand on her knee again as if reassuring himself that she was really there.

By half past eight it was already warm and Jenny was beginning to feel drowsy after the late night and early start. "We'll stop for breakfast in a few minutes," said George as she gave a big yawn.

Huts on either side of the road showed that they were approaching the outskirts of a small town. They slowed down as a couple of ragged boys vainly tried to keep their herd of cattle from straying on to the road.

"You wouldn't think this was one of our major highways," said George as one of the animals defecated unceremoniously right in front of them.

"Are there any plans to tar it?" asked Jenny as they made their way slowly past the cows. She coughed as the dust that was being kicked up by their hooves covered the truck. George quickly wound up his window and Jenny did the same. Immediately the heat inside the cab seemed overwhelming. George opened the small air vent and a whoosh of dust came in and burnt their nostrils.

"I believe there are plans to tar as far as here," he replied winding his window down as they passed the last of the cows. "It shouldn't be too difficult to here, but the next hundred and fifty kilometres is through thick sand which will double or treble the cost. And there aren't any more towns between here and Fort Joan, just a few villages."

Jenny felt a thrill of expectation at George's words. Once past this town she would really be venturing into the African wilderness.

"We'll take a break now," said George as he manoeuvred the vehicle across the road and down a turn-off to the right.

They drove slowly past the low white buildings of the police station where the police were having their morning inspection. The Charkian flag had already been raised and was fluttering in the light breeze. On the other side of the road was an old colonial style double storey building with a notice outside saying District Commissioner's office. Next to that was a primary school and, as they slowed to avoid a pair of donkeys standing obstinately in the middle of the road, they heard chanting from some of the classrooms.

They came to a halt by a petrol pump and Jenny saw with surprise that they were parked on the dusty forecourt of a small filling station.

"This is the last filling station until St. Joan but they often run out," said George as he jumped out of the cab. Jenny felt her heart start to race as she watched him walk round the front of the truck to her door. As he opened the door for her their eyes met and Jenny once more felt a surge of passion. She felt she couldn't wait until they had reached their destination. For a moment they were motionless as they gazed at each other trying to fight back their desire. A whimper suddenly distracted their attention and they looked down to see a small white dog nosing around George's feet. It looked up at them with its head to one side as if it understood what was going on, then with a dismissive air it shuffled away to the huge front wheel, cocked its leg, urinated on the tyre and trotted off with its tail in the air.

Once again their eyes met but now they were brim-full with laughter. George held out his hand and Jenny jumped to the ground chuckling and pointing to the little dog.

A young man dressed in blue overalls walked languidly over to them. He responded to George's greeting with a mournful shake of the head indicating that there was no petrol.

"Not to worry," George looked at Jenny reassuringly, "we've got more than enough in the spare drum."

"I wasn't worried," said Jenny, her eyes dancing as she looked at the peeling notice over the shop proclaiming Joe's Garage for all Motor Spares and at the sullen youth tossing an empty cigarette packet on the ground.

George studied Jenny's radiant face for a moment then he said, "There's a restaurant over there near the market. I'll just move the truck away from the petrol pump and we'll walk."

Jenny wandered across the road and paused in front of a young man who was sitting sewing a pair of trousers with an old treadle machine. His quiet absorption in his work seemed to emphasise his good looks. As he answered her questions Jenny was suddenly reminded of James and wondered with a pang why she hadn't seen him since the party. She frowned slightly then turned and her face lit up again as she saw George crossing the road towards her. He greeted the tailor politely then slipped his arm possessively through Jenny's and guided her down the street.

"Mm, that makes me feel hungry," she said as the smell of frying meat wafted towards them. They passed a woman crouched by a fire grilling pieces of meat on wooden skewers.

"It probably smells better than it tastes," laughed George. "I've found from experience that you need iron teeth to eat grilled mutton."

They walked on a little further then came to a small single storey house slightly set back from the street. Jenny was surprised when they entered to see that it was just a small poorly-lit grocer's shop with the usual selection of tinned fish, corned meat and packets of tea and sugar. The young girl behind the counter with her intricately-plaited hair, smooth complexion and chic white blouse looked out of place amidst the boxes of mosquito coils and her cheap biscuits. She greeted George like an old friend and Jenny looked at her suspiciously for a moment. The girl must have sensed Jenny's unease for she held out her hand in welcome and with a friendly smile said that she would tell her father they were there. She turned and went, leaving the door at the back of the shop open and Jenny caught a glimpse of a shady courtyard and some flowers that reminded her of roses. George leant easily against the counter and in a few moments an elderly Charkian appeared.

"Ah, Mr. Farrier, you are welcome," he said shaking George's hand enthusiastically.

"Winston, I'd like you to meet a very special friend of mine," said George with a touch of pride as he introduced Jenny. "Jenny, this is Winston, the best cook in Chark. Winston can you make an extra special breakfast for us this morning?"

Winston's bright eyes looked shrewdly from George to Jenny and he said with a flourish, "You shall have breakfast fit for a king and queen."

Jenny felt a thrill of anticipation as Winston led them past the cartons behind the counter and out of the door at the back.

They found themselves in a small mud-floored courtyard enclosed on three sides by the shop and two other buildings and on the other by a mud wall on which patterns were picked out in white, red and ochre dyes.

There were a couple of wooden tables and chairs but what caught Jenny's eye were the tubs of flowers.

"But they are roses!" she gasped bending over and burying her face in the rich pink blooms.

Winston watched her appreciatively then hurried back into the shop and returned with a packet of safety pins. He carefully selected a large rose-bud, took a penknife from his pocket and cut the rose from the bush. He then trimmed off the thorns and presented it to Jenny together with the safety pins.

"Oh thank you," she said flushing with pleasure. She looked at the rose and then at George who took it from her and pinned it just above her breast.

"Please sit down," said Winston pulling out a chair for Jenny. "Elizabeth will bring you some water while I prepare breakfast."

As he went towards one of the rooms Jenny noticed that he walked with a pronounced limp.

"What happened to him?" she asked.

"He was wounded fighting for the British at Tobruk." George laughed at the surprise on Jenny's face. "It's true! Soldiers were recruited from all over Africa and it was largely as a result of seeing how Europeans really lived that the independence movements got started. Winston was invalided out of the army with a small pension, he returned to his home town and has been a grocer ever since. But he picked up some new ideas when he was in the Mediterranean and so this restaurant is something different."

Jenny nodded and looked at the roses. "And his name? Surely that's not a coincidence?"

"No. Apparently the people called him Winston when he returned from the war. This was only a village in those days and he was treated as a real celebrity."

At that moment Elizabeth appeared with a white table-cloth over her arm and carrying a tray with water jug and glasses. She put the tray on the chair while she spread out the cloth, then she set out the jug and glasses, gave a quick smile and disappeared.

Jenny sat back contentedly sipping the cold water while George told her stories of how he used to accompany his father and Jenny had a picture of a kindly man very similar to George. She wanted to ask about his mother but everything was so perfect and she intuitively felt that his mother was a subject he didn't wish to talk about.

"Do you always stop here?" she asked instead.

"I often call in for a cup of coffee but I'm usually in too much of a hurry to stop while Winston prepares a meal. Today's different," he added taking Jenny's hand.

She sighed contentedly. She had the feeling that she was suspended in time. Neither the past left so recently behind or even the unknown future ahead were important. Her senses were all trained on the present. She sat quietly absorbing the warmth of the sun on her shoulders, the feel of George's firm hand covering hers, the sounds coming from the street outside and the delicate fragrance of the flower at her breast.

Elizabeth came again with the tray. She put a plate with half a pawpaw in front of each of them. The fruit had been scooped out then put back in with fresh pineapple and guavas. There was half a lemon on each plate.

"This looks lovely," said Jenny squeezing lemon over the pawpaw.

When they had finished Elizabeth reappeared with two bowls of sorghum porridge. It was the first time Jenny had tried soft porridge and she found she enjoyed the nutty flavour. The final course was boiled eggs with toast and a pot of fresh coffee.

Winston joined them as they were drinking a second cup of coffee and Jenny asked him about his war experiences. It was some time before George reluctantly got up and said that they had to be going. He paid the bill, thanked

Winston for his hospitality and then he and Jenny walked back through the shop and into the street.

"We're later than I planned," said George as they walked towards the truck, "but I think it was worth it."

"Oh yes, it was lovely meeting Winston and you're right about him being a good cook."

They reached the garage and climbed into the truck then headed out of the town and back on to the main road. George had to drive more carefully due to the thick sand. On the few occasions when they met a vehicle travelling in the opposite direction, their vision was obscured by clouds of yellow dust.

They had been travelling steadily for about an hour when they saw a donkey cart coming round the bend towards them. Suddenly a land-rover appeared as if from nowhere behind the cart. It was on their side of the road and hurtling straight towards them.

Jenny gave a little scream and braced herself for the impact. George wrenched the steering wheel hard to the left and pulled the truck off the road just as the land-rover thundered past, missing them by a hair's breadth. The cattle truck ploughed on into the bush and ground to a halt as it hit a fallen tree.

"Well," whistled George still clutching the steering wheel, "that was a narrow shave. Are you alright?"

"Yes, fine," said Jenny with a determined smile. She wondered why her legs looked normal when they were shaking so. Tentatively she opened the door and jumped out. The dry grass pricked her feet through her sandals and she made her way slowly round to the other side of the vehicle, her legs still trembling like jelly.

George had got out and was leaning against his door gazing at the cloud of dust getting smaller and smaller until it was only a speck in the distance. "He was in a mighty hurry," he said shaking his head. "I wonder why he didn't stop. It's unusual on this road. People normally stop if you're in trouble, they know it's a long way from anywhere and you never know when you might be the one needing help yourself. You see what I mean," he finished as the driver of the donkey cart came up to them. The four donkeys waited patiently, their heads bowed in an attitude of abject servility, while their master looked at George's truck straddling the fallen tree and shook his head in sympathy.

George bent down and looked underneath the truck. The man squatted next to him and also peered under the vehicle. Then he stood up and spoke rapidly in Chakari indicating that they should dig around the trunk.

George hesitated. "I'm tempted to see if we can move without digging. The crucial point is whether the tree has punctured the sump." He put his head under the vehicle again. "It's difficult to tell what's happening under there at the moment. Let's see if I can move it."

He got in and revved the engine but the vehicle refused to budge. "Okay then we'll just have to dig," he said getting out again.

The man brought a spade from his cart and started to shovel vigorously. George looked at him for a moment then he took a spade from the back of the truck and followed suit.

"Can I help?" asked Jenny.

"It's okay, there's only one spade."

Jenny watched as George swung the spade easily to and fro. His body was relaxed and he made the operation appear effortless. He seemed oblivious of the sun beating down on his golden hair or of a small spider exploring the freckles on his deeply-tanned arm.

After a while he walked to the front of the truck and cleared away some branches that were on the ground. Jenny and the driver of the donkey cart waited as George got back into the driver's seat.

"Well, here goes. Stand well clear," he shouted as he started to rev the engine. The engine roared, the tree groaned. Jenny held her breath as the truck rocked back and forth and then with a sudden lurch it was over the tree. George steered along the path he had cleared and was then back onto the road.

"Hooray!" cried Jenny and clapped her hands in excitement.

The man smiled and shook her hand and they both walked quickly to where George was parked by the side of the road.

"It seems to be okay," grinned George. He offered Jenny the water flask.

"That's better," she said taking a sip and handing it back. George took a mouthful then passed the flask to their companion. He held his head back and poured the water without it touching his lips.

"That's clever," murmured Jenny.

George thanked the man for his help, they shook hands and then George and Jenny got into the truck and continued slowly along the road.

They had been travelling for about half an hour when the oil warning light came on.

"That's ominous," said George quietly. "I topped up the oil this morning. We shouldn't need any for a long time yet."

He slowed down and came to a halt. There was no shade and the sun beat down fiercely on their backs as they bent over the engine.

When George pulled out the dipstick it was practically dry. He shook his head as he wiped it clean. "We'll have to take it very easy from here," he said. "I'm afraid we've got a small oil leak."

He fetched a container from the back of the truck and carefully poured some oil into the engine.

"Let's see how long that lasts," said George as he put down the bonnet.

He put his hands on Jenny's shoulders. "I hope you're not worried," he said anxiously.

Jenny laughed. "I'm enjoying every minute of it."

"I believe you really are," George said half incredulously. "Oh Jenny, just wait till we get to Rossano, I've got so much to show you. I'm sure you'll love it."

"I'm sure I will too."

"Tell me about your grandfather," she said when they were in the truck again.

George reflected for a few moments before starting the tale.

"Thomas Farrier was a corporal in the British army during the Boer War. He was very taken with Africa and was lucky enough to be with one of the regiments that remained after the war was over. After he had served twelve years he left the army hoping to make his fortune. But even then work wasn't easy to find. Anyway he managed to get a job as a transport rider travelling with the ox wagons that took supplies from the coast up to the gold-fields on the Highveld. He enjoyed travelling in the bush and wanted to see more of Africa. He gradually made enough money to run his own transport company bringing supplies to this part of the world. Fort Joan was the end of his route and it was there that he met and married Maria Benoni the daughter of a farmer who had emigrated from Southern Italy. Maria was the only surviving child and her father didn't want to lose her. Besides that he had taken a liking to his son-in-law so he suggested that he could manage the farm. This gave him time to experiment with his vineyards so they were both happy. Thomas started breeding cattle and became quite successful in a small way."

George paused for a moment before continuing, "Yes, he was successful in breeding cattle but not children. My father Alfie was the only child to survive infancy. My grandmother died in childbirth with her fifth child. It was a tough life for women in those days."

"It still is for many women," said Jenny thinking of Mrs. Ntoo's daughter as she had crouched in the dark hut waiting uncomplainingly for her baby to be born.

"Was your mother also a farmer's daughter?" she asked. George sighed. "It would have been better if she had been," he said bitterly. "No, my mother was the daughter of Mr. English, the District Commissioner. And she was English through and through."

Instinctively Jenny brushed her hand across George's forehead to smooth away the unaccustomed frown that had appeared. His fingers that had suddenly gripped the steering wheel too tightly relaxed and he took Jenny's hand and squeezed it.

"Your grandfather must have had some fascinating experiences when he was travelling with the ox wagons," said Jenny.

"He did. And I used to love to sit and listen to his tales when I was a kid."

For the next half hour Jenny sat spellbound as George recounted some of the stories that his grandfather had told him of his encounters with wild animals, of fording rivers in flood with a full span of oxen and of involvements in inter-tribal skirmishes. He was in the middle of describing a visit his grandfather had made to the Ntisi king in Mutape when the oil warning light flashed on again.

"This looks like being a long trip," said George as he brought the vehicle to a halt again.

He finished his story while they sat by the side of the road waiting for the engine to cool down. Then he poured in more oil and they continued on their way driving even more slowly than before.

An hour passed and then the tell-tale light flashed again.

"I guess I'm going to have to fix it," said George dropping the speed to a jogging pace. "So we'll find somewhere comfortable to stop."

He carried on until they came to a track going off to the left. George swung the vehicle off the road and along the track for about five hundred metres. There were bushes on either side and Jenny looked about wondering where they were going to stop.

Suddenly the bushes finished and they found themselves looking over a shallow valley. Two tyre tracks could be seen running across the short grass until they disappeared from sight in the trees at the further end of the valley.

As they watched a giraffe appeared from behind a lone tree to the left. It walked gracefully over the short grass, pausing to sniff suspiciously every now and again, until it finally merged with the trees on the other side of the valley.

"Oh, isn't he beautiful! Will we see any more?" Jenny looked eagerly about her.

"We're more likely to see zebra. But you can never tell what you'll see. Now why don't you sit and look while I see if I can fix this oil leak."

George got out of the truck and started rummaging through his tools. Then he lay under the vehicle and expertly ran his fingers over the sump.

"Can I do anything?" asked Jenny.

"You can get the torch. It's in the glove compartment."

It took George some time to locate the leak but he finally found it half way up the sump.

"That's got it," he said.

"Good, But how can you fix it?"

"I've got some epoxy putty but it must be thoroughly cleaned first. It won't stick if there's any dirt or oil."

George picked up a handful of sand and rubbed it over the sump.

"It's a pity we haven't any Vim," said Jenny.

"That's clever of you. I bought some in Munari because you can't get it in Fort Joan. It's in one of the carrier bags at the back."

Jenny found the Vim and a cloth which she dampened and handed them to George.

"Thanks. That should do the trick."

He worked steadily for a few minutes then he scratched the surface deeply with his penknife.

"Now for the putty." George two equal pieces from the bars and kneaded them together until they were well mixed. He then lay under the truck again and pressed the putty firmly into the dent.

"Let's hope this works," he said as he stood up.

"Do you think it will?" asked Jenny anxiously.

"It should do. In any case we'll have to give it a couple of hours to set before we can continue."

Jenny looked taken aback but said quickly, "It's a beautiful spot to wait in."

"Yes, it wouldn't have been much fun on the side of the road. Now let's see about making a fire then we can have a cup of coffee."

There was plenty of dry wood around and they soon had a fire blazing.

"I always keep some emergency supplies," said George taking a small and very battered tin trunk from the truck. He took out a billy can which he filled from the water container that was built into the back of the truck.

"Are you hungry?" he asked indicating the tin cans in the trunk.

"You really are prepared," laughed Jenny. "But I'm not hungry. That was such a good breakfast."

They drank their coffee then Jenny jumped up and looked at the valley stretching out before them.

"It's cooling down now. Let's go for a walk," she said taking George's hand.

As they strode out across the grass Jenny felt a sense of freedom surge through her once more. It was years since she had walked without being accompanied by one or two small children dragging her back or pulling her forward in a direction she didn't want to go.

They walked for over an hour swapping experiences of hill-walking in England and Wales and bush-treks in Chark.

When they got back to the truck they flung themselves down near the remains of the fire feeling both tired and stimulated with the exercise.

The passion that they had kept in check throughout the day could no longer be controlled and they made love wildly, caressing and crooning in their ecstasy, until they finally lay entwined around each other in an exhausted sleep.

Chapter Twelve

It was dusk when Jenny awoke. For a moment she studied George's face, gently tracing his blonde eyebrows with her finger. She ran her hand through his thick tousled hair but that did not wake him so she quietly got up, made herself presentable and went over to the truck. She took the blanket that had covered the seat and lay it over George then re-lit the fire, filled the billy can and put it on the fire to boil.

She stood leaning against the truck looking out across the valley but turning every now and again to look at the sleeping figure on the grass. She heaved a sigh of sheer satisfaction; if they could remain here together for ever life would be perfect.

There was movement in the bushes and a small buck appeared, its nostrils quivering as it looked around before walking timidly across the track just a few metres in front of Jenny. She stood perfectly still even after it had disappeared from sight and when she turned to look at George once more he was watching her.

He held out his hand to her and her body was immediately aflame as she cast his blanket aside and fell on top of him. Fleetingly she was amazed and slightly frightened by the intensity of her passion but then she was oblivious of everything but her need to consume and be consumed by the man for whom she had given up everything to be with. It was the hissing of the water as it boiled over on to the fire that brought them back to reality. They laughed delightedly like small children caught being naughty while doing something exquisitely pleasurable. They got up, dressed themselves and made the coffee, giggling and keeping close to each other the whole time. Then they sat down, their bodies still touching as they sipped their coffee and watched the last streaks of gold and crimson fade in the sky.

"We must be sensible for a moment and think," said George.

"But I always am," objected Jenny.

"Yes, so am I. And I'm realising it's not a good way to be year in and year out." George sighed then smiled at Jenny. "How would you like to spend a night under the stars in the African bush?"

"It sounds idyllic, provided the company's right."

"I can guarantee the company. To be honest I'm not suggesting this entirely for romantic reasons. I'm still worried about that oil leak and I don't know whether the putty will stop it. If it had been earlier I would have been willing to risk it but I don't want to be stranded on the road in the dark."

"Then we'll stay. I'd rather arrive in daylight anyway." Jenny looked keenly at George. "You don't look too certain about it though."

"No, it's fine. It's just a pity we couldn't have got back before dark as planned. I should have paid my workers today as it's the last Friday of the month."

"Oh dear. Will it matter?"

"As long as we're back by midday tomorrow it should be okay. It's never happened before and they're a nice bunch. It would be a different matter if we were dealing with the army."

"What do you mean?"

"Pay week-end in a town where the army are posted is quite an event. I've heard that in Mutape they march the soldiers into the bush and pay them there."

"Whatever for?"

"In the past all their creditors in the town, especially the bar owners, used to wait outside the barracks and as soon as the soldiers came off duty they would demand their money. Often the soldiers refused to pay and then there were all kinds of fights. This way there are no big confrontations but there are still a lot of angry creditors."

"It's a good job you're not employing the army then. How many workers have you got?"

"Six permanent people and I employ casual labour when it's necessary. In the old days farmers would employ as many as a hundred man to work in their fields and they would bring their wives and children and they'd all live crowded together in a native village. Some of the more philanthropic farmers even built schools for "their" natives but that didn't happen very often."

George picked up a piece of wood and threw it on to the fire. "If we're going to stay we'd better collect some wood; it's best to keep a fire burning all night. I'll just get the torch so we can see what we're picking up."

They found a dead branch and dragged it near the fire. Jenny held the torch while George lopped off the outside branches with an axe and then pushed one end of it into the fire. They carried on steadily piling more sticks on to the woodpile. After about ten minutes George stood back and said, "That's fine, there's enough there to see us through the night."

"Is it going to get so cold?" asked Jenny innocently.

"Cold? Oh no," George laughed. "The reason people always have a fire at night is to scare away the wild animals."

"Oh!" Jenny shivered suddenly, then quickly bent down to stoke the fire in an effort to hide her fear.

George squatted down beside her. "Don't worry Jenny. There are no lions in this area. But there might be the odd leopard about so it's best to be on the safe side. And you're right, it will keep us warm. One blanket and a sleeping bag between us isn't going to be a lot of protection against the night air."

He stood up and, pointing to the old tin trunk with a flourish, said, "Shall we select tonight's meal?"

The next couple of hours passed pleasantly as they pottered about. The food was not particularly appetizing but they were hungry and in a mood to find everything enjoyable. There was no moon but that served to make the stars brighter and George pointed out some of the constellations. They walked a little way into the valley to get a better view and Jenny felt a sense of awe as she looked at the myriad stars shining, some of them hundreds of light years away.

When they returned to the camp they made their bed and Jenny felt suddenly shy as they discussed which side they liked to sleep. She found herself thinking that what had started out as a romp had now turned into something serious. But it always was serious, she told herself, shocked that she could think otherwise.

Once in bed, however, her fears vanished as they gave themselves up to a slow melodious love-making knowing that they had the whole night ahead of them.

. . . .

George was already up when Jenny awoke. The sun had not yet risen and the air was chilly. She pulled the covers tightly around her. George, however, seemed unaffected by the temperature. He was stripped to the waist and washing vigorously in cold water. He greeted her merrily then proceeded to shave, peering at himself in the wing-mirror of the truck.

Jenny felt she should get up but was loathe to leave the warmth of the sleeping bag.

George must have guessed how she felt. "Don't get up," he called. "The water's nearly boiling. I'll bring you a cup of coffee."

Neither of them felt like sampling the tinned food again for breakfast so they made do with two cups of coffee and a packet of biscuits.

George checked underneath the vehicle and to his relief there was no oil to be seen.

Jenny took a last nostalgic look at the valley then climbed into the truck, George swung it round and they headed back on to the main road.

Fortunately, George's fears had proved unnecessary and they made steady progress along the dirt road which, apart from the odd donkey cart, was practically empty.

For the first couple of hours the land was flat and the vegetation a monotonous scrub growing close to the road. Once they passed a troop of baboons playing by the roadside but, apart from that, there was little sign of life.

Jenny was beginning to wonder what sort of place they were going to when suddenly the landscape changed. The scrub gave way to pasture on which were scattered traditional compounds. Herds of goats were grazing and people could be seen working around the compounds. A couple of children ran and waved as they saw the truck approaching. Jenny smiled and waved back then turned her gaze past George and out of his window.

On the horizon were the mountains. The huge rocky outcrops loomed purple in the distance. They did not appear to form a continuous range but their contorted forms looked as if they had been dropped by some angry god during creation. Even from that distance they looked both forbidding and compelling and Jenny felt a surge of excitement as the road brought them gradually closer.

"My farm's in that direction," George pointed and looked at Jenny with a touch of pride mixed with uncertainty.

"We could take a track across from here and by-pass Fort Joan but I'm sure you'd like to see our "big city" first."

Jenny leant forward, all her senses alert, now that they were nearing their destination.

They rattled over a bridge, perilously narrow and with nothing to stop unwary vehicles from plunging over the side.

The houses on either side of the road were set well back and more spread out than those in Bambo. A number of the buildings were made of concrete blocks with tin roofs but the majority were mud and thatch. They slowed down as they passed the carcass of a dog lying in the road. Jenny averted her gaze and looked ahead of her wondering when they were going to come to the centre of the town. She glanced at George who seemed to be looking at the familiar sights with satisfaction.

"We're just coming up to the police station on our right," he said. Then he braked suddenly, throwing Jenny forward as he did so.

"What is it?" she asked looking in bewilderment at the empty road.

"Look!" he pointed agitatedly. They were stopped directly opposite the police station. The flag pole was in the middle of the parade ground and the Charkian flag was flying at half mast.

It was a moment or two before Jenny comprehended the enormity of the situation. "What does it mean?" she asked softly as a gradual feeling of unease began to sweep over her.

"I don't know," said George gravely. "We'll stop at the post office and find out."

They drove on slowly past a couple of closed shops until they came to what George euphemistically described as the town centre comprising the post office, library, bank and a few small shops. People were standing about in small groups but no-one appeared to be going in or out of any of the buildings. When they looked more closely they saw that everything was closed.

George looked at his watch. "That's odd. It's only half past ten. Everything should be open on a Saturday morning." He stopped the truck and leant out of the window scanning the faces hoping to see someone he knew.

"George!" came a shout and a Charkian came hurriedly towards him.

"Elijah!" said George holding out his hand. "What has happened?"

The man took George's hand and looked up at him. He was silent for a moment, then said solemnly, "The President has been assassinated."

"Jesus!" exclaimed George and slowly released his hand. "When did it happen?"

"Five o'clock yesterday evening. The rebels have control of the radio station and they have imposed a dusk to dawn curfew."

"Has there been much fighting?"

"The news bulletins don't say much. They just tell everyone not to panic and to stay in their homes for the week-end."

"Well that's what we'd better do. Thanks Elijah. Take care."

George started up the engine, took one last look at the sombre crowd and then drove slowly away.

"Welcome to Fort Joan," he said ruefully taking Jenny's hand and squeezing it.

Jenny looked at him with wide eyes not trusting herself to say anything. For the first time since she had left home she thought of Darren and David. A sharp pain pierced her chest and she drew in her breath sharply as she realised that they might be in danger.

"I wonder where it happened?" she heard herself say in a high-pitched voice.

"He was due to open the new sports centre in Mutape yesterday. My guess is that it's a Ntisi organised coup."

Jenny nodded mutely.

"I don't think we'll have anything to worry about here," continued George. "Most of the people here are neither Ntisi or Funi. It's a bit like Bambo," he continued shrewdly, "the people there don't have any strong allegiances to either of the major tribes and as there is no army barracks there it won't be strategically important."

Jenny smiled gratefully and felt her pulse-rate slowly return to normal. She looked out of the window and tried to blot out images of Darren and David that kept dancing before her eyes.

They had turned off the main road and were travelling along a rutted track heading towards the mountains. The sun was shining and, now that they were nearer, the peaks seemed smaller and less forbidding.

Jenny wanted to ask how much further it was to Rossano but she still didn't trust herself to speak naturally. She looked down at her feet, grimy with the travelling, and thought that it would be good to have a bath. As she looked out of the window again she saw a girl standing with a bucket on her head. A thought suddenly struck her. Maybe George didn't have a bath. Maybe he didn't even have running water. Perhaps she would have to fetch water. But she didn't think she would be able to carry a heavy bucket without spilling it. Even if she did she wouldn't manage it with the grace of the Charkian women. Unconsciously she knit her brows into a frown and tensed her body as she imagined what it would be like to carry a bucket of water on her head.

Sensing her change of mood George said, "I expect you're tired after the long journey. We'll be there in about twenty minutes."

Jenny nodded then asked, "Where do you get your water?"

"From the river that forms the eastern boundary to the farm. The problem is that it doesn't flow all the year but my great-grandfather had a well dug near the original house. It's still there but we only need to use it on the rare occasions when the pump breaks down."

"The pump?"

"My father had a bore-hole sunk directly into the river bed. So we have a continuous supply of water in the house."

Jenny nodded again and smiled.

George slowed down as they came to a village. Most of the dwellings were traditional huts but there were one or two modern houses. They passed the primary school and came to a halt a little further on outside a small white-washed house with a tin roof set in the centre of a round courtyard surrounded by a low mud wall. Hollyhocks were growing up one wall of the house and near the back of the compound Jenny could see a small vegetable patch covered with twigs. A couple of young trees were also protected by small branches and when Jenny saw some hens scratching about she realised why.

"I won't be a minute," said George getting out. He took a box from the back of the truck and went to the front door of the house. An old woman came out and, speaking to her in Chakari, George handed her the box. Jenny was too far away to hear what they said and her attention wandered to the children playing hide and seek among the thatched huts in the next compound. Suddenly they all ran out and into the old woman's compound. The children were all shapes and sizes but it was a little girl of about three years old that particularly took Jenny's attention. She had always been fascinated by people's different shades of skin colour and it amused her to hear them described as "that black man" or "the yellow man". This child was a striking copper colour and her soft brown curls framing her face made her body seem minute in relation to her head. The children surged round George and the old woman, and Jenny could no longer distinguish the little girl. She saw George gesture to the old woman who delved in the box and held up a packet of sweets. The children chattered and giggled excitedly while she ceremoniously divided the sweets among them. George disentangled himself and strode back to the truck. As he drove away he waved and hooted to the children who waved back and ran behind laughing until the truck was moving too fast for them to follow.

149

They drove out of the village and followed a fence on their left-hand side. "That's the McDougal's farm," said George as they passed an imposing gateway. "They're our neighbours."

Jenny leant forward trembling in anticipation. Any moment she expected to see the farm of which she had heard and dreamt so much. However it was another five minutes before they passed a fence going at right angles to the one next to the road.

"That's our boundary." George gave Jenny a sidelong glance and they continued in silence until they came to another gateway.

"Here we are," he said as he turned the truck then came to a stop. "I'll get out and open the gate."

"No, let me," said Jenny and jumped out. The gate was in need of a fresh coat of white paint but it opened easily. As George drove through Jenny gave a mock bow then pushed the gate closed, fastened it carefully and ran back to the truck.

Cattle were grazing in the fields on either side of the road. the scene looked so peaceful that Jenny found it hard to believe that in another part of the country the President had been shot and many others probably lay dead and wounded. She quickly banished the thought from her mind and looked ahead straining for her first glimpse of the farmhouse.

The road went up a slight incline. George braked when they reached the top and waited with the engine still running.

"Oh!" gasped Jenny. "It's lovely."

At the bottom of the rise was a long low white-washed farmhouse. To the right and slightly in front were some barns. To the left was an orchard. The ground behind the house sloped down to a wide sandy river bed. What looked like a series of high hedges went from the house to the river then Jenny realised they were vines. On the other side of the river the land rose steeply. The massive rocks had been weathered into an amazing variety of forms. Some were vast and smooth like a gigantic slide. Others were jagged and impenetrable. The diversity of colour from the lichens covering the surface and the clumps of vegetation springing from many hidden clefts gave life to the old grey rocks. Perched on top of one of the rock slopes was a boulder that had been weathered in such a fashion that it looked human in form.

"That's our wise old woman," said George following Jenny's gaze. "The belief is that as long as she remains in place no harm will come to the valley."

He took his foot off the brake and drove slowly down the incline, coming to a halt at the side of the house. George switched off the engine and jumped out of the truck but Jenny sat motionless looking straight ahead of her, trying to comprehend that her journey was at an end.

She turned as George opened her door and held out his arms to her. "Welcome to Rossano," he said tenderly as she took his hand and jumped from the truck.

Chapter Thirteen

Pink and cream hollyhocks bobbed in the light breeze by the front door.

Jenny was surprised to find that it did not open directly into a room like all the other Charkian houses she had visited but into a small hallway. There was an old carved chest against one wall and a small Japanese table with mother-of-pearl inlay by the arch that led into the passage. The floors were of highly polished parquet. George turned left and Jenny followed him into the last room on the right. It was a large airy bedroom. Giving a cursory glance at the double bed, Jenny walked straight to the window.

"What a beautiful view," she said leaning against the window sill and looking out at the garden running down to the river and the hills beyond.

"It's lovely isn't it. I moved into this room soon after my father died because of the view." George glanced at his watch. "I think I should let Innocent know I'm back and pay the men. Would you like to have a bath?"

Jenny caught sight of herself in the gleaming mirror and nodded.

George went back into the passage. "That's my old bedroom," he said pointing to the door opposite. "The bathroom's next to it and the toilet is next to that." He paused uncertainly. "Just make yourself at home. I won't be long."

Jenny went back to the bedroom and stood for a moment trying to get her bearings. The carpeted floor and matching bedspread and curtains gave the room a sophistication that seemed out of keeping with George's open down-to-earth character. There was a wash basin in one corner of the room and Jenny washed her hands before unpacking her things and laying them on the bed.

She went to the bathroom and smiled at her fears that she would have to carry water herself. There was plenty of hot water and even a mixer tap and shower attachment. On the bathroom shelf was a bottle of shampoo, some afterimage and two jars half full with purple and green crystals. The jars had lids with old-fashioned glass stoppers. Jenny took off the lids and wondered whether she should use the crystals. She sniffed but they had no scent. They must be very old she thought as she put them back on the shelf.

After her bath Jenny went back to the bedroom and wondered what to do next. Although George had told her to make herself at home she felt it would be impolite to poke about on her own.

She decided to go outside.

George and a Charkian man were sitting on a bench near the back door. They were in earnest conversation but they both looked up and smiled when she appeared.

Even before they were introduced Jenny guessed that the man was Innocent, George's foreman. He was about the same age as George, shorter but just as powerfully built. "We've been talking about the coup," said George then looked at his watch. "It's nearly twelve o'clock. There should be a news bulletin. Shall we go inside and listen? Innocent will you come?"

Innocent nodded and George led the way into the lounge. Like the bedroom it faced the garden and the hills beyond and there was a door at one end opening on to the verandah. Jenny sank down in an armchair facing the view. George switched on the radiogram then disappeared into the kitchen. The room was suddenly filled with the sound of military music. Jenny opened her mouth to say something but the pensive expression on Innocent's face stopped her. Jenny could hear George talking to someone in the kitchen and she wondered if he would be long.

She sat quietly taking in her surroundings. The white walls were in need of a coat of paint, the Indian carpet worn and somewhat faded but the furnishings had obviously been chosen with care. On the wall next to the fireplace was a brass warming pan and standing in the hearth was a set of fire implements and a toasting fork. A pair of tarnished silver candlesticks and a silver rose bowl stood on the mantelpiece. There was a glass-fronted china cabinet containing a Royal Albert tea service, a set of Venetian glasses and a collection of glass ornaments. On the top of the cabinet stood an ornate Italian clock. There were two book cases. One was full of the Encyclopaedia Brittanica. Two shelves of the other were taken up by the distinctive patterned covers of the Companion Book Club popular in England in the 1950's. Jenny was just going to get up to look at the other books when George appeared. He stood for a moment in the doorway. Jenny looked at his unkempt hair and weather-beaten features and was puzzled. He seemed out of keeping with the refinement of the house. She glanced around again and caught sight of a water colour of Salisbury Cathedral. Then she realised: it wasn't George that was out of place but the house itself. The military music stopped and they listened in silence as the news reader announced that Chark was now a People's Republic. They were told that they had been liberated from a corrupt regime and that in the future there would be a more equal distribution of resources. Finally they were told that, for their own safety, they should remain in their homes as much as possible and in any case everyone should observe the dusk to dawn curfew.

"Let's see what the World Service has to say," said George as he started to re-tune the radio.

"........ing is continuing in the two main cities in Chark," declared the BBC news reader in dispassionate tones. "All borders have been closed and the radio and telecommunications are still held by the rebel forces. The earthquake in Peru........"

George switched off the radio. "Well Innocent, what do you think?" he asked.

Innocent shook his head. "I think it's bad. I know there's been corruption and we Ntisi have been exploited for many years but I don't think that violence is the answer." He sighed and the expression of anger and frustration on his face fleetingly reminded Jenny of James.

She had a sudden picture of a small boy running from the rest house towards her followed by an even smaller boy trustingly holding the hand of a Charkian who had been her friend. A feeling of desolation swept over her as she realised that things would never be the same again. But isn't that what you wanted? her other voice asked. You said you couldn't go on with things as they were.

She looked up and saw that George was watching her. Their eyes met and they smiled, oblivious for the moment of Innocent's presence, the coup or anything except each other. Slowly George turned to Innocent and said, "I asked Rebecca to prepare some lunch. Will you join us?"

"Thank you, but I will go home now." Innocent stood up. "Goodbye Jenny. I look forward to seeing you again on Monday. Goodbye George."

They followed Innocent to the door and then went into the kitchen.

Jenny had expected a traditional farmhouse kitchen but was only partly surprised by the modern fitments and black and white tiled floor. It was an airy room with windows along most of one wall looking out on to the road leading down to the house. The side door was thrown open and a large grey cat lay basking on the step. The table in the centre of the room was set for two.

"The soup's from a tin I'm afraid," said George as they sat down, "but the bread's fresh; Rebecca said she made it yesterday."

"Has Rebecca worked here for long?"

"All my life. She was my nanny," said George simply.

After lunch George took Jenny for a tour round the farm in his old short-wheel based land-rover. She was pleased to be out of the house where she had felt strangely uncomfortable. George too became more animated as he pointed out familiar land marks. They drove back up the rise and along a sandy track that was fenced on both sides. At the end of the track was a gate and an old man wearing baggy shorts and a torn shirt waved and opened it for them. They were in a kraal and George stopped the land-rover and got out. Jenny followed and looked around. Even to her inexperienced eye the cattle seemed in better condition than those they had passed along the road. George introduced her to the old man and then asked him some questions in Chakari. He seemed relieved by the answers and, turning to Jenny, said that everything had been well during his absence and they were waiting for one of the cows to give birth in the next day or so. He moved among the cattle, speaking to some by name and rubbing his hand over their flanks as he checked to see that nothing was wrong. The pregnant cow was lying under a large acacia tree and George squatted down to speak to her encouragingly, stroking her as he did so. "We'll have to keep an eye on her, we were up all night last time she calved," said George giving her a final pat before walking back to the land-rover. He had a few more words with the old man who then opened the gate at the other end of the kraal and they drove on.

They passed a couple more kraals, empty but obviously recently used, and George explained how he rotated the cattle to make best use of the pasture. Every now and again he stopped and they got out. Sometimes it was to check the fencing, sometimes simply to show Jenny an unusual flower or point out some feature of the landscape that had particular significance for him. Once he stooped down looking intently at the ground and showed Jenny some spoor. It had been made by a cloven-hoofed animal but was larger and more splayed than a cow's footprint. "Wildebeest," he announced grimly and explained what a pest the ugly creatures were because they spread diseases amongst the cattle.

Jenny was fascinated by everything she saw. She found it invigorating to be away from the confines of the hospital compound and the demands of her two small children and she found it exhilarating to be with a man whose zest for life and obvious delight in her company gave her back her sense of self-esteem which she had lost somewhere since coming to Chark.

The afternoon passed quickly and Jenny was surprised to see that the sun was low in the sky as the farmhouse came into sight again at the bottom of the rise. George parked the land-rover and they were greeted by a tempting aroma as they walked into the kitchen through the open back door. Rebecca was busy at the sink and she turned and welcomed Jenny kindly.

After their meal they listened to the news but there was no change. They took their coffee on the verandah and watched the stars until they both started to feel sleepy. Then, laughing slightly self-consciously, they agreed that it would be best if they had an early night.

. . . .

Sunday was spent in a leisurely way. After a late breakfast George put his rifle in the land-rover and drove to where they had seen the wildebeest spoor the previous day. They got out and followed the spoor through the bush for over an hour. Once they disturbed a duiker crouching in the undergrowth but they saw no trace of wildebeest. Jenny was secretly relieved; the prospect of shooting wild animals was not one that appealed to her.

In the afternoon they walked down to the dry river bed. There were some rocks in the middle and George told Jenny how they used to dive into the water from the highest rock when the river was in flood.

"And this is where we had our secret camp," he said taking Jenny's hand and crossing to the farther bank.

"We?" said Jenny questioningly as they started to walk along a narrow path, but George did not hear.

"This is it," he said as they came to a couple of large boulders. There was a hollow between them filled with dead leaves. "It doesn't look much does it." George sounded let-down. "But the rest of it's gone now. We made another room coming out here, it even had a thatched roof. Oh well - it was a long time ago." He stepped forward and Jenny thought he was going to kiss her but his eyes looked past her as if he was trying to focus on something that was just out of sight.

Jenny suddenly felt very alone. She looked back across the river at the farmhouse and outbuildings. She saw the trellised vines that Mr. Benoni had planted to remind him of his native Italy. She had a sudden vision of his dark-haired daughter strolling along the river bank with Thomas, her English lover. A rustle in the bushes made her start, she felt suddenly disorientated. The image of Thomas and Maria had taken hold of her imagination and she found herself looking inside the house. Maria, ten years older, was lying in bed. Her black ringlets clung to her pallid forehead, her breathing came in shallow gasps and her dark eyes were clouded with pain and despair.

"Oh no!" cried Jenny involuntarily and clasped her hand over her mouth.

"What is it Jenny?" George's anxious voice brought her back to reality.

Jenny shivered and gave a false laugh. "Nothing. I think I had a hallucination."

George took her hand and the warmth comforted her. They walked back along the path and across the river. There were a lot of questions Jenny wanted to ask but George was absorbed with practicalities. They stopped to check that the water pump was working properly, then spent a while in the vegetable garden. They picked a lettuce, a couple of ripe tomatoes and a large, shiny green pepper. When they returned to the house Jenny prepared a salad to eat with their supper. Before the meal they fed the cats and closed the chicken house then went to the little shed in which the generator was housed. It needed more diesel so George filled it up and showed Jenny how to switch it on. It was old and temperamental and Jenny was glad that she didn't have to contend with it on her own. George paused as they walked back to the house.

"What is it?" asked Jenny as he hesitated.

"I'm worried about our expectant mother up in the kraal. I know she was okay when we passed this morning but I think I'd like to check. Do you mind?"

Jenny's stomach rumbled and she realised the fresh air had made her hungry. "No of course not," she said brightly. They got into the land-rover and drove quickly away from the farmhouse and towards the setting sun. When they arrived they found that the cow was perfectly alright but George took his time as he examined her then made a brief inspection of the other cattle in the kraal. He gave instructions to the old herdsman to call him at the first sign of trouble, they exchanged pleasantries in an unhurried fashion for a few moments longer then George and Jenny got into the land-rover and drove back to the house. The hum of the generator greeted them as they got out and strolled towards the open kitchen door.

George explained that Rebecca did not usually work on a Sunday but she had come in that morning specially to prepare a meat loaf for their supper. Jenny murmured her appreciation. She felt like an honoured guest but silently asked herself if that was what she wanted. What was her position here anyway she wondered. Her eye caught sight of some old cookery books she hadn't noticed before and for a moment she felt like a usurper in another woman's kitchen.

She was quiet as they ate their meal and was glad that George was in a talkative mood. He expanded on the problems - and joys - of owning a farm in this part of the world and she listened with the same serious concentration that she had used to listen to Richard when he told her about his successes and failures in the hospital.

When they had finished their supper they went into the lounge and George turned on the radiogram. They were too late for the seven o'clock news and Jenny for her part wasn't interested. A sense of unreality threatened to overcome her. The feeling was particularly strong when she was in the lounge. Sometimes she could almost feel the indefinable presence of the woman who was responsible for the careful decor of the room. She intuitively sensed that George's mother must have been a strong woman but the room also gave her a feeling of discordance, her overwrought nerves seemed to jangle if she stayed there longer than five minutes.

George switched off the radio and they carried their coffee on to the verandah. Jenny felt herself relax as she looked out into the darkness although her sense of unreality remained. The hallucination she had had of Maria came back to her and she had an urgent need to know more about the women who lived in the house before her and in particular about George's mother.

"George," she began hesitantly, then stopped to listen as they heard the sound of a vehicle approach.

"That sounds like Will McDougal's bakkie," said George half-apologetically. "You remember we passed his farm on our way in yesterday. He and his wife were friends of my parents, although they were quite a bit older. They used to play whist together every Sunday. They were very upset when my father died. Then Will's wife died last year and he became a bit of a recluse. It's only recently that he's started calling round again."

They heard a door slam and heavy footsteps coming along the side of the house to the verandah. An elderly ruddy-faced man appeared wearing an ancient tweed jacket, baggy corduroy trousers and well-polished black boots. He stopped and stared in surprise when he saw Jenny.

"It's good to see you Will," said George getting up and ushering the old man to a chair. "I'd like you to meet my friend Jenny. Jenny, Will McDougal."

Will grasped Jenny's hand firmly though he looked at her a little warily.

"Would you like a some scotch Will?" asked George.

"Aye, just a wee drop son," said Will, his blue eyes twinkling.

"And you Jenny?"

"Yes please." She felt like saying "a double" but restrained herself. She slapped a mosquito that had settled on her leg and tried to overcome the feeling of resentment that her quiet evening with George had been shattered.

"Where are you from?" asked Will when George went into the house to fetch the drinks.

"Pardon?"

Will looked at her keenly and repeated the question.

"Oh." Jenny was at a loss for words. Where was she from? Not from Bambo surely? Or London? Or was it Middlesex?

"I'm from England," she said after a while.

"England." Will nodded reflectively. "You a friend of Maria's?"

"Maria?" whispered Jenny her eyes wide with incomprehension.

"Maria'd be about your age," said Will looking at her thoughtfully.

For a moment Jenny had a crazy feeling that she was in a time warp and had slipped back eighty years. Then George arrived carrying a tray with three glasses, an ice bucket and a bottle of scotch.

Jenny's hand shook as she took her glass.

"Cheers," said Will raising his glass to Jenny. "To an enjoyable holiday. You staying long?"

"It's difficult to make any plans at the moment with the coup," said George skilfully diverting the subject.

They talked about the political situation though Jenny said little. Will's last question kept echoing in her mind. How long was she staying? When she walked out of her house on Friday morning she had believed she was going for ever. But what did George think? It was a subject they hadn't cared to talk about.

She drained her glass too quickly but George just winked at her as he refilled it.

The conversation turned inevitably to their farms and Will told Jenny how he had been struggling to make a living on a small croft in Ross and Cromarty when his father's unmarried brother died in Chark leaving his property and all his possessions to Will. "All his debts more like it," chuckled Will wryly. "Helen and I were courting at the time, it was the 1930's and prospects at home were grim so we decided to try our luck here. We got married by special license and set sail immediately. And we never regretted it." Will drained his glass for the third time. George lifted the bottle to refill the glass but Will stopped him. "That's enough son. It's time I was getting along." He heaved himself out of his chair. "Thanks son. And don't forget to bring the young lady to see McDougal's farm soon."

Jenny and George accompanied Will to his bakkie and then walked back to the house with their arms around each other in the darkness.

The urge to ask questions had left her. All Jenny wanted was the assurance of George's body next to hers. She wanted to be roused then soothed into a state of oblivion. A state where neither the past nor the future existed. A state where no questions were asked and no judgements made.

Chapter Fourteen

Jenny awoke the next morning and stretched out her arms towards George. He was not there. She sat up staring wildly around her, her heart beating frantically in fear that he had left her.

Even though the curtains were closed the glare of the sun behind them made her blink. She screwed up her eyes and looked at her watch. It was a quarter to nine. Slowly her heartbeat returned to normal. Of course, it was Monday and George started work at half past six. He must have tiptoed out in order not to wake her. She smiled at his thoughtfulness but wished that he had taken her with him. She did not know what she was expected to do here on her own.

Mechanically she got out of bed and dressed. She could hear someone in the kitchen and thought joyfully that George had returned. She almost ran down the passage and into the kitchen then stopped dead still. Rebecca was standing at the table squeezing oranges. Jenny drew in her breath. "Good morning Rebecca," she said as calmly as she could.

The old woman smiled. "Good morning madam. The master said to tell you he's in the kraal and he'll be back for breakfast at ten o'clock. Shall I make you a cup of coffee?"

Jenny nodded. "Thank you. If it's no trouble."

She wandered out of the door and looked up at the hills. The brilliant blue of the sky gave the old woman of the valley a clarity that was both comforting and disturbing. Jenny wondered how long she had been there and how long she would remain.

She felt something warm brush against her legs and a half-grown tabby skittered at her feet in a playful fashion. She bent down to stroke it but it was semi-wild and ran off.

Rebecca appeared at the doorway holding a mug. Jenny took it and sat down at the kitchen table. She cupped her hands around the mug more for comfort than warmth. When she had finished she went to the bathroom then wandered into the bedroom. She sat on the bed wondering what to do. She wanted to go for a walk but she was afraid she would meet someone. The look of surprise on Will McDougal's face the night before had unnerved her.

"Make yourself at home," George had said when she first arrived. Well then, she would.

She went into the passage and looked at the closed door next to the bedroom. Then, feeling rather like a thief, she quietly opened it and went in.

It was another bedroom, smaller than the one she shared with George. Along one wall was a single bed covered with a pink candlewick bedspread. There was a pink rug on the floor and the floral curtains were predominantly pink. The kidney-shaped dressing table was fringed with the same floral curtains. The walls were bare and so was the inside of the wardrobe. Jenny peered into the mirror and, in her heightened state of awareness, half-expected the face of the former occupant of the room to look back at her. "Who are you?" she asked. But the face in the mirror threw the question back to her.

Jenny stood for a moment longer, gazing unseeing at her own reflection, then tiptoed out of the room quietly shutting the door behind her.

She stood hesitantly outside the next door and then boldly opened it. In the centre of the room was an Ercol dining suite, 1950's style but looking like new. There was a Wedgwood fruit bowl on the sideboard and a framed black and white photograph. Jenny picked it up then took it to the window to get a better look. It was a family group taken when George was about twelve by the look of it. His father was instantly recognisable, he had the same warm smile as George though his features were heavier, more

Italian. His hand rested on his wife's shoulder but she seemed unaware of it as she sat with straight back and head erect looking directly at the camera. Her fair hair was piled into a chignon and there was a single string of pearls around her neck. She was a striking-looking woman but she seemed out of place next to her husband and son. Jenny had saved her scrutiny of the fourth figure till last. It was a girl, about eight years old and, although her curly hair and eyes were darker than George's, her nose and jaw were similar and her smile as she looked at the camera was George's smile.

Jenny frowned and gripped the photograph as she studied it. "Who are you?" she whispered for the second time that morning.

She looked out of the window. She could still see the old woman of the valley but there was a cloud behind her now and from this angle her features seemed distorted.

Jenny shivered and walked back to the sideboard. She replaced the photograph and walked out into the passage. She stood for a moment looking at the closed door of George's bedroom. But she had done enough poking about for one morning.

Avoiding the kitchen, she let herself out through the hall and sat on the bench outside waiting for George to come. She had a lot she wanted to ask him. Did he have a sister? If so, why did he never mention her? He had said that the McDougal's were very upset when his father died, but what about his mother? Why did he mention her so rarely?

Jenny sat contemplating these questions until she saw the land-rover rattling towards her. George smiled as he got out of the vehicle and gave her a quick kiss but his face was preoccupied as he strode into the kitchen, washed his hands at the sink then sat down to breakfast.

"How's the cow?" asked Jenny stealing herself not to ask the questions that were uppermost in her mind.

"Not too good I'm afraid. I'll have to drive to Fort Joan and get the vet. Normally I could phone but of course the lines are down. Blast this coup!"

Jenny had never seen George so agitated. For a moment he reminded her of Richard when he was confronted with an incurable case.

She helped herself to a small bowl of porridge but she wasn't very hungry. The fresh orange juice was refreshing and she managed to eat a fried egg but she did not fancy the liver so early in the morning. She was astonished at the amount that George was able to eat until she reminded herself that he had done nearly half a day's work already.

When they finished George got up and said, "Are you ready then?"

"Oh yes,"said Jenny gratefully. From the way he had spoken earlier she had thought he was going without her.

A few minutes later she was sitting in the land-rover feeling the wind rush past her as they sped along the track and out of the farm back along the road to Fort Joan.

In less than twenty minutes they were parked outside a small building labelled veterinary department. George strode in and spoke rapidly to the girl sitting behind a typewriter. She shook her head and George let out a gasp of annoyance.

"He's been called out to Pala Ranch," he said turning to Jenny. "That's a good twenty kilometres west of here. Anyway Grace is going to give him the message as soon as he returns."

He smiled at the typist and walked towards the door seemingly unaware of the fluttering of her eyelashes and thrust of her chest as she said goodbye.

Jenny gave her a tight smile but Grace ignored her as she gazed at George's departing back.

"What will happen if the vet comes too late?" asked Jenny as they drove back out of town.

"Innocent and I will probably manage, we have before," said George stretching his arms as he held the steering wheel. He reduced his speed and Jenny looked about her with interest.

They went slowly through the village where George had stopped on Saturday. As they passed the old woman's house the little girl that Jenny had noticed before ran to the gate and waved. She was wearing a bright yellow dress that looked new and she had a yellow ribbon in her hair. George slowed almost to a standstill and waved back.

"What a pretty child!" exclaimed Jenny as she too waved. George flushed and gave a strange smile, half pleased and half sad. He opened his mouth to say something and then closed it again. He accelerated and they drove rapidly away from the village.

When they got back to the farm they drove straight to the kraal.

The cow was standing forlornly under the acacia tree anxiously tended by Innocent and the old herdsman who was rubbing her belly and speaking encouragingly in a low sing-song voice. As they approached the cow looked at them and moaned.

George bit his lip and hurried forward with an expression that once again reminded Jenny of Richard. He asked a few questions then walked briskly to the standpipe, rolling up his shirt sleeves as he did so. He washed his hands and arms thoroughly in the cold water and shook them to dry. Some of the droplets landed on Jenny and she shivered though it was more tension than cold.

George thrust his arm up to his shoulder into the cow's womb. The animal gave a piteous moan as George exerted all his strength in an attempt to turn the calf into the correct position.

"Got it," he panted removing his arm and letting the viscous liquid drip onto the ground. "Now we must just let nature take its course."

He went back to the tap and washed his arm again.
Jenny stood transfixed as the cow heaved and groaned.
She felt totally helpless as she watched the three men
making encouraging sounds and stroking the tired beast.
Suddenly there was a bellow of anguish and the calf's head
and feet emerged. They all held their breath and waited
expectantly. There was another bellow and part of the
calf's body became visible.
Jenny smiled with relief but a look at George's face
showed her that it was too early for rejoicing. The cow
groaned again but this time the calf did not move. Again
and again the mother attempted to expel its calf but it
remained where it was wedged in the birth canal.
Finally George took hold of the calf's feet and pulled. It
came suddenly like a cork out of a bottle then toppled and
fell to the ground. George bent down to see if it was
breathing, shook his head anxiously, then picked it up by
its hind legs and swung it like a pendulum in an attempt to
start the breathing. He then placed it on the ground and
looked at the mother.
The cow bent down and sniffed the calf, moaned, then
turned away.
Grimly George once again picked it up by its hind legs and
swung it to and fro. Then he put it down again and felt
anxiously for its heart beat.
Jenny could tell from the expression on his face that there
was none.
As George, Innocent and the old herdsman conferred in
Chakari, Jenny felt excluded. She wished there was
something she could do to help but she could tell that at
that moment George had no need for her. His whole being
was involved with the suffering cow and her stillborn calf.
"Would you like me to go back to the house and fetch you
all something to drink?" volunteered Jenny for the sake of
something to do.

"There's water here," George said shortly. Then when he saw the hurt look on her face he added, "But why don't you go and get yourself a coffee, I expect you could do with one. I'm okay, you get used to this kind of thing on a farm."

But Jenny could see from the grave expression and dejected stoop of his shoulders that this was an aspect of farming that one never got used to. Just as Richard never got used to his patients suffering although he hardened himself to it.

Slowly she turned away and walked towards the farmhouse.

Everything was quiet when she arrived. She made herself a cup of coffee then went to the lounge and switched on the radiogram. It was a relief not to be greeted by military music but there was too much interference to hear anything on any of the stations.

She wandered aimlessly back to the bedroom feeling let down. She felt very much in need of positive information particularly after her discoveries that morning.

She went into the passage and looked across at the closed door of George's room. Without further thought she opened it and went in. She closed the door behind her and felt suddenly enveloped by George's presence. A leopard skin covered the bed and an air rifle leant casually in one corner of the room. On top of the bookcase was an intricate model of a galleon in full sail and a tractor made out of meccano. The books were an assortment of school text books, boys annuals and a few natural history books. There were several framed certificates on the wall above the bookcase, mainly for swimming but also his matriculation certificate. On the wall by the bed was a pen and ink sketch. When she looked more closely Jenny could see it was a view of the river and mountains taken from the house. Each feature was carefully drawn and the whole picture captured the essence of the place. Jenny wondered if George had done it but the initials were M.F. That rang a bell somewhere but Jenny was unable to work out why. She gingerly opened the wardrobe and stepped back as the smell of moth balls pervaded the room. It was crammed with George's old clothes, including his school uniform, several pairs of boots, a train set and some games. On the top shelf in a glass-fronted steel case was the rifle that George had taken the day before.

Jenny closed the door and turned her attention to the dressing table. It was piled high with papers and, not wanting to be too nosey, she was about to move away when she noticed the photographs. One was a framed black and white photo of an attractive young African woman holding a baby carefully wrapped in a lacy shawl. The other was unframed but in colour. Jenny picked it up to get a better look. It was a close-up of a little girl standing in front of a land-rover. Her copper-coloured skin and soft brown curls looked familiar. It was the little girl who had waved to them that morning.

Slowly Jenny put the picture back. She peered at the African woman with the baby and nodded at her. Then, with a last glance at the copper-coloured child, she left the room.

She took a bottle of beer from the fridge and walked round the outside of the house to the verandah. She was unaware of time passing as she sat watching the shadows lengthen on the hills. She did not even hear George's footsteps some time later and started in surprise when she saw him standing in front of her. He looked strained after his ordeal and Jenny was at a loss for words.

"Did you hear any news?" he asked.

"News?"

"On the radio."

"Oh. No, I couldn't hear anything at all."

George looked at his watch. "It's nearly six o'clock. I think it's worth trying again."

He went into the lounge and tuned the radiogram, then called excitedly, his head close to the set. The reception was still very poor but they could just make out the voice of the Vice-President. He told the nation that government forces were in control and the rebels were in hiding. He said that the curfew was still in force and that no-one was to travel on the main roads without a pass from the military. He ordered anyone who knew of the whereabouts of any of the rebels to report the matter immediately to the armed forces or the police. Finally he declared that the nation would be in mourning for a month due to the death of the President.

They went into the kitchen for their supper and George talked about the possible consequences of the coup for the country. He hoped that there wouldn't be harsh reprisals because it would only make the Ntisi more embittered. They had probably hoped for support from the Ntisi on the other side of the border in Tambalia but it had obviously not been forthcoming.

After they had finished their meal they took their coffee as usual to the verandah but a cool wind had suddenly sprung up from the east and they found it too cold to dawdle there. They returned to the lounge and sat in the armchairs on either side of the fireplace. George fetched a bottle of wine and two crystal goblets while Jenny sat with her face cupped in her hands staring at the logs in the hearth in readiness for the short winter.

"What music would you like?" asked George as he flicked through the records.

"I don't mind. You choose."

"I haven't listened to this for ages. It was my father's favourite." George took The New World Symphony out of its cover and put the record on the turntable. He handed Jenny a glass of wine and she sat back with her eyes half-closed as she listened to the music.

"My father was fond of classical music too," she said after a while. "He belonged to a record club. Where did your father get his records from?"

George frowned. "It wasn't my father who collected records. It was just that he liked The New World. My mother used to get so annoyed with him. She could accept that he wasn't interested in ballet music but she could never understand why he didn't like Beethoven's Pastoral."

"And why didn't he?"

"He said it was too soft. I think he thought it trivialised nature."

"But your mother wasn't soft," said Jenny before she could stop herself.

"Not on the outside. But inside she was different. And when she sat listening to music, especially if my father wasn't around, she lost the severe expression that people found so forbidding." George sighed. "It's only very recently that I've realised how unhappy she was."

They simultaneously sipped their wine and were silent for a moment.

"When did she die?" asked Jenny sympathetically.

"Die?" George almost shouted the word, then spoke more calmly. "But my mother isn't dead. She's living in England." He paused as if searching for words to continue.

"With Maria?" asked Jenny softly.

"Yes," said George with relief. "How did you know?" Jenny told George what Will had said and about the photograph in the dining room.

"But why did you never mention her?" Jenny was genuinely puzzled.

George brushed his hand through his hair in a distracted way. "It hurt too much," he said simply.

He poured himself some more wine and sat back in his chair looking at Jenny all the time as he spoke.

"It was twelve years ago now. Maria had just turned eighteen and I was twenty-two. Maria and I had always been very close - brothers and sisters tend to depend more on each other in this type of situation. But I suppose she wasn't suited to the life as I was. It was lucky for me - and for my father - that I always wanted to be a farmer. Maria didn't really seem cut out to be a farmer's wife. But she wasn't the career woman type either. She was just very nice, everyone liked her." George paused and sipped his wine. "She was artistic too."

Jenny nodded remembering the sketch in George's room. "Things hadn't been right between my parents for years though I didn't notice at the time because they didn't have rows. My mother ran the business side of the farm very efficiently and encouraged my father to experiment. He made quite a lot of money and he let her spend it how she wished. I'm sure he loved her very much and he was desperate to make her happy. He had the house renovated for her - the kitchen, bathroom and my room were added on twenty years ago. And she insisted on having a hallway with a parquet floor. It was terribly expensive. She was always sending to England for things and once Maria showed talent for drawing she spent a lot of money on art materials for her."

George raised his glass to his lips and then continued. "She wanted us to go to school in England but we were quite scared at the idea. My father didn't want us to go either and to be honest I don't think they could have afforded it. I went to St. Marks Academy in Mutape and Maria went to the convent there. A lot of boys I was at school with are in top government posts now. It was a really good school, we had all sorts of extra activities and there must have been boys from at least twenty nationalities. Maria's school was a lot more restricting. There were only about a hundred students, very few African though quite a few Indians. My mother was always complaining about the narrowness of the curriculum. And by the time she reached the sixth form I think Maria found it rather frustrating. My mother tried to get my Dad to discuss Maria's future but he couldn't see there was any problem. And at the time neither could I. I hadn't been a problem you see. All I ever wanted to do was work on the farm with my Dad."

"So what happened to Maria?" asked Jenny breathlessly as George drained his glass and then refilled it.

"She and Mum always wanted us to go to England for a holiday but of course you can't just go away from a farm. And anyway my father didn't want to go. I was twenty-two then and it was beginning to penetrate my thick skull that things weren't too good between Mum and Dad. So I suggested that the three of them went on a grand tour. I was quite capable of running the farm by that time and Will would have given me a hand if I had needed it. But Dad refused to go. It's funny you know, he gave my mother everything except the one thing she really wanted. I'll never forget the look on her face when she realised that there was no persuading him. I can remember her words now. She said "If I go without you, you'll never see me again. I'm not going to allow Maria to be buried alive as I have been all these years." Then she gave up talking about going on holiday and cabled a friend to send details of art colleges in London."

George sighed and stared at Jenny. "And even when they were packing Dad didn't believe that she meant it. I remember him asking her when they were coming back and she nearly screamed at him "We're not coming back." It was a sort of desperate scream. I'm sure if he had tried to understand even then things might have been different."

"But what did Maria think?" asked Jenny.

"She was really excited about going to art college. And she'd never been out of Chark before so she didn't realise what a big step it was. She said to me when they left, "See you in three years," just like she used to say to Mum and Dad, "See you at the end of term" when she went off to boarding school."

"But why hasn't she ever come back?"

George shrugged. "You know how it is. You get busy and the years slip by. I suppose it was partly my fault. I'm not a good letter-writer at the best of times and I was so bitter with them both for leaving us that I didn't want to write. My father was distraught when it finally sunk in a couple of days after they'd gone that it really was for good."

"But why did she do it like that? I mean how could she just leave you?"

George looked at her sadly. "It's quite easy isn't it?"

Jenny sat looking into his sad honest eyes. She felt sick. She wanted to run and hide. But she couldn't move. She looked away but all around her she could see things that had been left behind by a woman who had fled in her despair.

Inevitably her eyes were drawn back to George who was still looking at her steadily. "Why did you let me do it?" she whispered.

George was silent for a moment as he attempted to find the right words.

"Because I loved you," he said simply. "And I still do," he added as he saw the look of disbelief on Jenny's face.

"And I suppose you reminded me of Maria, she had your enthusiasm for life. When I asked you to come with me I didn't believe you would say yes although I knew you were unhappy."

"But weren't you worried about the boys?" Jenny wanted to say then stopped herself. I'm being ridiculous, she thought; the boys are nothing to do with George, they're my responsibility. Mine and Richard's. For the first time since leaving Bambo she consciously allowed herself to think about her sons. What are they doing? Were they missing her? What had Richard told them? Who was looking after them? Richard had said he would be off duty on Friday, Saturday and Sunday. But even when he was off duty he usually called in to check his cases. And who had looked after them today? And what about the rest of the week? And the following week?

Tentatively she looked at George. " Will McDougal asked me how long I was staying. What did you think?"

"I didn't know. I didn't dare think about the future. I just thought I'd enjoy the present while it lasted."

Jenny nodded slowly in agreement.

Suddenly she found the atmosphere stifling. She stood up. "Let's go for a walk," she said.

It was cold outside and they walked briskly hand in hand towards the river.

A crescent moon could be seen amid the stars. Breathing deeply Jenny gazed up at the sky searching to find some meaning hidden among the constellations. But the wine, mixed with the fresh air and the sudden output of emotional energy had made her muzzy.

She put her hands up to George's face and stroked him as if to make sure he was real. Gradually she caressed the rest of his body and suddenly they were on the ground and making love rapturously. By this time their ecstasy was tinged with sorrow as if they both sensed that their days together were numbered.

Chapter Fifteen

Darren and David are walking along a dirt road hand in hand together. There is bush on either side and not a soul is in sight. Suddenly a donkey cart appears from nowhere and comes clattering down the road towards them. A man sits on the cart and lashes the donkeys with a long whip. As they draw parallel to the little boys the man leans across and flicks his whip towards them. It curls around their bodies and with a malevolent grin Jonah, for it is he, pulls in his catch wriggling soundlessly like fish at the end of a line. Jenny puts out her hands to save her sons but Jonah lets out a blood-curdling cry and the cart disappears in a cloud of dust. In its place sits Richard all alone on the top of the hospital hill. His hair has turned white and his brown eyes are full of pain as he beckons to Jenny. She lifts her foot to take a step forward but she is unable to move. She makes one tremendous effort to reach her husband and then feels herself falling down, down. She is lying at the foot of some scaffolding on a building site in London. She looks but the body on the ground is not hers, she is some distance away and looking at her brother-in-law Bill's crumpled body. She runs forward to help him but as she bends down next to him she sees that it is James lying in a pool of blood. He is trying to give her a message but she does not hear because Darren and David are calling to her in the distance. She tries to get to them but the way is strewn with rocks. She starts tearing at them with her bare hands in her frenzy to get to her children.

"Jenny!"

Gradually Jenny felt the familiar warmth of George's body beneath hers, they were in his bed and Jenny was sprawled on top of him. Bewildered she sat up and George lit a candle that was on the bedside table. He put his hand to his face and rubbed it. Jenny looked at the scratch on his cheek with incomprehension then at the three parallel scratches on his chest.

"That must have been a really bad dream you were having Jenny," said George ruefully as he gently massaged his chest.

"Oh my God. It was terrible," Jenny sobbed and buried her face in George's shoulder.

"What happened?" he asked stroking her hair with one hand and rubbing his chest with the other.

"It was the boys. I was trying to get to them. There were rocks in the way. George - I'm so sorry," said Jenny looking at the wounds she had inflicted.

"The boys are alright," he said comfortingly. "I'll go and put the kettle on for a cup of coffee."

"Was the dream only about the boys?" asked George when he came back.

"No. For a moment I thought I was Bill."

"Bill?"

Jenny told George about Bill's accident and the effect it had had on Richard's family.

"We'd often talked of going abroad," said Jenny reflectively, "but there were always reasons for putting it off before."

The piercing whistle of the kettle sounded through the silent house and George hurried back to the kitchen. He came back with two cups of coffee and the bottle of whisky.

"I didn't know you were a midnight tippler," said Jenny with a brave attempt at a laugh.

"Oh yes, the wardrobe's full of empty bottles," George grinned. "Seriously, would you like a drop in your coffee?"

Jenny nodded. The liquor revived and relaxed her.

"I was so upset when you told me your mother was still alive," said Jenny before she had time to think about what she was saying.

"Why ever was that?"

Jenny looked confused. "I'm sorry. That was very tactless of me. It's just that, up until then, I thought you were an orphan like me."

"Do you think of yourself as an orphan?"

"Only when I'm feeling very sorry for myself. I never was one anyway because I was eighteen when my father died."

They sat in silence for a while drinking their coffee.

"George," said Jenny urgently taking his hand. "I've got to go back."

George put his empty cup on the table. "Let's talk about it in the morning. Would you like some more whisky?"

She shook her head.

"Do you think you'll be able to sleep alright now?"

"I think so."

George blew out the candle and drew Jenny to him.

. . . .

Once again Jenny woke to find herself alone in the bed. She got up and dressed quickly. She felt surprisingly refreshed and chatted cheerfully to Rebecca as she made herself a cup of coffee.

When she had finished she decided to walk to the kraal to see if George was there. The morning air was cool and she walked briskly enjoying the song of the birds and the wind in the trees. As she passed an ancient marula tree she was startled by a raucous caw and looked up to see a couple of lowrie birds perched on a branch. "Go away, go away," they cawed and Jenny remembered that they were often called the "go away" bird. "It's alright, I am going," she said to the birds half-expectantly, half-regretfully. As she stood looking up at the tree George's land-rover came rattling down the road and drew to a halt beside her. She turned and saw his tanned face smiling at her and she felt her resolution weaken. She couldn't leave this man who loved her so much and in whose company she felt so totally at ease.

"How are you feeling this morning?" he asked as Jenny got into the seat beside him.

His words brought back the nightmare that she had been trying to erase from her memory and she saw, as clearly as if he were actually there, Richard beckoning to her and heard the shrill voices of her children calling her.

With a great effort she said. "I'm alright thank you. But I meant what I said about leaving. How's your chest?"

"My chest? Oh!" George laughed then squeezed Jenny's hand. "Don't worry about that."

Jenny drew in her breath. Would she really have the strength to go back? Since coming to Chark Richard had rarely tried to understand her fears. She remembered him rushing off importantly to the hospital the day after she had killed the owl. It had been George who had taken the trouble to listen to her and comfort her. Ever since Bill's accident, Richard had always seemed to be hurrying away from her. Wouldn't it be just the same if she went back? And anyway would he want her back after the way she had left him? And what about the boys? Would they despise her for having left them?

George pulled to a halt at the side of the house and looked at his watch.

"It's nearly nine o'clock. Shall we see if we can get the latest news?"

They went into the lounge and George switched on the radio. The reception was better than the previous day and they listened attentively. The government announced that the rebels had been completely routed and most had already been taken prisoner. People were sternly informed that there would be severe penalties for harbouring dissidents and anyone with any information of their whereabouts should contact the police or military immediately. Border posts an all main roads were still closed and the dusk to dawn curfew was being strictly enforced.

Jenny looked at George after he had switched the radio off. "How am I going to get back?" she whispered.

"Jenny it's not safe to go yet. Things should be better by next week; if you still feel the same then...." George swallowed hard then finished almost inaudibly, "you can go then."

"Next week?"

But the boys need her now. Or was it Richard who needed her? She looked out of the window at the mountains and she knew with an intensity that startled her that her way lay eastward across the Vandu.

"I've got to go immediately, I have this overpowering feeling that one of them is in danger. And the news said that it's only the main roads that are blocked," Jenny said still looking towards the mountains.

George got up and paced the room, his faced creased with pain at the thought of losing her. He turned and shouted at her in anguish. "Jenny, you can't go that way. It's just the place where the rebels will be hiding."

She shrugged her shoulders and said nothing.

George studied her face for a moment then said. "Do you really want to leave so much?"

"Oh God! I don't want to leave at all," she said desperately. "But I've got this terrible feeling that I must go before it's too late. And anyway it's not fair on you if I stay. I should never have come."

"Don't say that. It's been wonderful." George was silent for a moment as he tried to find words to express himself. He knelt down and took her hands in his. "Meeting you was like, like unlocking a door. You were so warm and gay I just wanted to be near you. That's why I stayed that Saturday for the party." He paused. "I never dared hope that you would feel the same way about me. You seemed so involved in caring for your children."

"Didn't it spoil the image a bit when I abandoned them?" demanded Jenny grimly.

George shook his head. "By that time I didn't care about anything except having you with me."

"So how's it going to be when I'm gone again?" she asked softly.

"Jenny, you mustn't go. Not now anyway, it's dangerous."

"But you do see that I must go back? Sometime?"

George sighed. "I can't force you to stay," he said softly. Jenny looked around the room with a mixture of sadness and irritation. Just as your father wouldn't force your mother. But her thought was unspoken.

"Do you still write to Maria?" she asked instead.

George got up and took two glasses from the drinks cabinet. He poured a generous amount of whisky in each, handed a glass to Jenny than sat down in the chair facing her.

"I haven't written since my father died. I nearly wrote when my daughter was born but I didn't know how they would take the news." George looked questioningly at Jenny to see her reaction.

"You mean the little girl in the yellow dress?"

He nodded.

"Where is her mother?" Jenny asked as matter-of-factly as possible in an urge to hide the irrational surge of jealousy she felt.

"She's a teacher in Munari although her home is here. We used to see each other when she came home for the holidays. But she wasn't interested in continuing the relationship after Rachel was born. To tell you the truth she hasn't shown a lot of interest in her. And now that she's planning to marry a man in Munari I don't think she'll even visit very often."

"Who looks after her?"

"Her grandmother. She's a very nice woman but she's getting old."

"Why can't Rachel come and live here with you?"
George looked at her eagerly. "Do you think she could?
Wouldn't it be bad for a little girl to be brought up by her
father?"
Jenny laughed. "It happens often in England. And you've
got so many advantages here, you've got Rebecca to help
you and you don't go away to work, you'll be able to really
get to know each other."
"That's certainly something to think about. Thank you
Jenny," said George simply.
Jenny said nothing as she thought about the pretty little
girl with the yellow ribbon. It would be nice to have a
daughter. If she stayed here with George............
"I'm hungry," she said abruptly as the smell of eggs and
bacon wafted from the kitchen.
"So Maria doesn't even know she's an aunty," reflected
Jenny as they ate their breakfast.
"No." George was silent for a while. "When...if...you
return to England, will you tell her for me? I want her to
know how much Rachel means to me. Though I doubt if
my mother would understand."
"She may have changed, people do you know."
"Maybe." George was thoughtful. "I think I understand
her a bit better now. But I wish she had come back to see
my father before he died."
"Maybe she wishes that too, maybe you're both waiting for
the other to make the first move."
George nodded and looked intently at Jenny as if trying to
find the answer written on her face.
"Let me give you Maria's address," he said haltingly. " But
in any case I shall write to both of them. You can't just let
a relationship fade away for want of trying."
"No," said Jenny, "you're right."
They ate the rest of the meal in silence each wrapped up in
their own painful thoughts.

When they had finished they went to where Innocent was fixing a leak in the water pipe.

"Innocent's a good mechanic," said George as he bent down to give him a hand.

Jenny stayed for a while watching them then wandered back to the house to wash some clothes. Rebecca had offered to do her washing but Jenny had felt that would not be right. She pummelled the clothes vigorously as she turned over and over in her mind the problem of how she was going to get back to Richard and the boys.

She was just hanging the washing on the line when George came over.

"Can you tell Rebecca to make some coffee. Innocent and I fancy a cup. We'll have it on the verandah."

Jenny was surprised. It wasn't long since breakfast. Before she could say anything George had turned away and was walking back towards Innocent.

Jenny went into the kitchen and put on the kettle. When it had boiled she called "Coffee's ready" and took the tray on to the verandah.

The two men joined her and for a moment they sat in silence. Then George spoke.

"I was telling Innocent about your premonition of danger. Or was it just a night-time fear?" he added hopefully.

Jenny shook her head vigorously. "It's getting stronger all the time," she said looking up at the old woman of the valley and the mountains beyond. "I know that it is imperative I leave here before I'm too late."

"We Africans believe in these things," said Innocent. Jenny thought he was going to say more but he sat back, his eyes half-closed and his knuckles taut as he gripped the arms of his chair.

George sighed and looked at Jenny. "If you really insist that it will be too late to wait until things have quietened down next week, Innocent is willing to drive you along the small roads through the mountains to Yonda. I have a friend who is a veterinary officer there and he should be able to help you."

Jenny looked at Innocent. His eyes were open and he gave a half-smile and nodded in agreement to what George had said.

"But, but you'll be putting yourself in danger," stammered Jenny. Up until then she had been thinking only of her need to get away but now that she was presented with a plan she could see why George had wanted her to wait. She was well aware that Innocent was Ntisi and she suspected that he harboured sympathies with the rebels.

"And you hardly know me," she added incongruously.

At that both men smiled.

"I must be crazy trying to help you leave," George turned suddenly to his friend. "And you're crazy too," he said desperately.

"It is as it must be," was the inscrutable reply.

"Then I'm coming too," George stood up and glared at them.

For a moment Jenny felt relieved, she wouldn't have to say goodbye after all. Not so soon anyway.

Innocent spoke evenly, "These are troubled times. There will be suspicions aroused if a Ntisi and a white man disappear together. And it is I who knows the mountains."

Jenny followed his gaze eastward and wondered what lay in store for them beyond the mountain peaks.

George studied her face willing her to change her mind.

"When do we leave?" she asked calmly.

He drew in his breath then said gravely.

"Innocent is prepared to drive as far as Yonda. If you leave early tomorrow morning you should be there well before night-fall even going the back ways. And as it's only the main roads that are closed you won't be contravening the law. If you are unlucky enough to run into a police patrol you can tell them the truth - -that you left Bambo for a short holiday with me before the coup and that your family expected you back on Wednesday. You didn't want to worry them so I sent you with my driver to see if you could get a lift from Yonda."

Jenny gave a wry smile at George's version of the truth. The three sat in silence for a while, each absorbed in their own thoughts. Jenny wanted to ask Innocent if he really meant what he said but as she glanced at his impassive face she realised the question would be foolish. He had said he was prepared to guide her to Yonda and he would. "Thank you Innocent," she said quietly. "What time shall we set off?"

Innocent looked questioningly at George.

"Five thirty should be early enough. You don't want to go before it gets light."

Innocent stood up and gave a fleeting smile. "Alright then Jenny, we'll leave at five thirty tomorrow morning. Is there anything you need for the journey?"

"Well, I suppose we'll need a little food and water," she said uncertainly.

"Innocent's going into Fort Joan now to get fuel and he'll see that you have enough provisions," said George. "We'll pack up the vehicle this evening," he added as Innocent took his leave of them and departed.

Jenny was going to remark that putting her old rucksack into the land-rover could hardly be referred to as packing up the vehicle but she thought better of it and said nothing. "I've got a couple of men mending fences on the northern boundary," said George. "Shall we take a run out and see how they're getting on?"

Jenny greeted the suggestion enthusiastically. She needed something practical to focus on to stop her thinking about her journey the following day.

They stayed out until late afternoon. It seemed strange that the places that George had introduced her to so recently she was now seeing for the last time. But that was something they did not dwell on.

When they returned the land-rover was parked but there was no sign of Innocent.

"He'll have gone home already. He'll need to be up early if he's to be here by five thirty," said George.

"Can't we go and collect him?" asked Jenny anxious not to cause Innocent too much trouble.

"It's best if you don't draw attention to yourselves. You're going to cross the river here instead of driving down to the ford. It's probably an unnecessary precaution but you can't be too careful."

"I'll be glad when it's all over," said Jenny fervently.

"You can still change your mind if you want to."

"No. Even though I've tried to put the feeling to the back of my mind it's been with me all day."

George sighed and held Jenny's hand tightly as they walked into the house.

. . . .

It was a cold grey dawn. Jenny couldn't help contrasting it with the gold and silver sky that held such promise as she had run to meet the man she loved only five days before. Then, she wouldn't have cared if the whole world had shared her joy. Now, she felt strangely reserved as she stood next to the land-rover and said goodbye to George for the last time.

They were both aware of Innocent already seated at the wheel staring at the way ahead of them. "Goodbye" they said in unison, looking quickly at each other then away again.

Jenny leapt lightly into the passenger seat and Innocent started the engine even before she had slammed the door. She looked ahead of her and wondered how they were going to get down the river bank and up the other side. Perhaps George would have to help them level the bank. Then she saw two planks leaning against the bank and Innocent skilfully manoeuvred the vehicle over them.

They crossed the river and drove up two more planks
similarly placed on the other side.

Jenny had been determined not to look back but, as they
passed the make-believe house where George and Maria
used to play, her resolution failed her. She looked and saw
George's powerful figure standing on the river bank,
motionless, as much a part of the landscape as the rocks
themselves.

"George!" she cried opening the window rapidly.

Slowly he lifted his hand to her then brushed it across his
eyes and let it drop limply to his side.

The land-rover veered to the right and George and
Rossano disappeared from sight.

. . . .

Briskly Jenny closed the window and searched for
something to say.

"I hadn't noticed the planks by the river before."

"I put them there yesterday. George will remove them so
as not to arouse suspicions," said Innocent looking straight
ahead of him.

Who would be suspicious? Jenny wanted to ask but she
kept silent and reminded herself that she was in a situation
of which she had no experience. Even now there could be
people watching them pass along the rocky track. People
who for generations had been suspicious of strangers
because they had learnt the hard way that strangers were
not to be trusted.

When the first white men had come to the Kingdom of the
Ntisi the king had made them welcome because he
believed the white men's promises that they would protect
them from the Funi who were threatening their southern
border. But the promises went unfulfilled and it was not
until it was too late that the Ntisi realised that the white
men had designs on the farmland of the Van flood plain.
Their king and many warriors were killed in battle against

a small unit of British soldiers and Ntisiland together with the area inhabited by the Funi became a British colony. Jenny knew that the Ntisi and Funi had traditionally been enemies and that the Independence Settlement was an outstanding example of bureaucratic ignorance. Not only were the two peoples joined to become one nation but the Ntisi tribe itself were divided between   Chark and neighbouring Tambalia. It was no wonder thought Jenny as the land-rover juddered along the seldom-used track that the Ntisi had rebelled, especially now that oil had been discovered in the flood-plain.

And where were the rebels now Jenny wondered as she peered into the thick bush on either side of the vehicle. Had they all been killed or captured or were some of them still in hiding? She tried to focus her mind on Richard and the boys but she was unable to form a clear picture of them. Despite that, the feeling that one of them was in danger hung over her like a dark cloud and she knew that her decision to leave Rossano had been right.

By nine o'clock Jenny's body was feeling jarred from travelling over the rocky terrain in the old hard-sprung land-rover. She was cold and looked in surprise at the clouds that covered the sky, she had thought it was too late in the season for rain. Many of the trees and bushes had already lost their leaves and the stark branches against the grey rocks and grey sky gave the landscape a forbidding appearance. Suddenly, the windscreen was spattered with raindrops, the sky became darker still and they found themselves driving through lashing rain. Without warning the track along which they were driving became a torrent and they slithered along while Innocent wrenched the steering wheel first to one side then the next.

Jenny looked at George's Ntisi friend holding on grimly to the steering wheel, his face puckered into a frown as he peered between the wiper blades. She shivered and wondered why he had come. It seemed strange that he

should embark on such a risky journey for the sake of a white woman's dream. Could she trust him Jenny wondered as the vehicle skidded around a double bend.
"Sorry," he said briefly as Jenny threw her arms in front of her and braced herself against the dashboard.
"You're a very good driver," she murmured weakly as she settled herself back in the seat and braced her body against any further skids.
For a while the track was straight although it seemed to be going slightly uphill. They reached the top of the rise and Jenny had just time to take in the swirling waters of a river only a hundred metres away. Then the vehicle slid rapidly down the muddy slope and ploughed into the dirty water. She dimly heard somebody, it must have been her, shout, "Brakes!" but was aware only of the beads of sweat glistening on Innocent's forehead and the whites of his eyes rolling in fear as he hauled on the steering wheel and finally brought the vehicle to a halt facing downstream. The river was not much more than a couple of cars lengths wide. Jenny leant out of the window and looked at the water churning around the top of the wheels and then glanced questioningly at Innocent.
He shrugged his shoulders. "There's nothing we can do except wait for the water to go down. If we are lucky it should only be a couple of hours, the water runs off very quickly after these flash storms."
But what if the storm continues and the level rises instead? Jenny wanted to ask. But even as she thought it she could see the rain has almost stopped.
"Well, I think you were due for a break," she said determined to be cheerful. "Shall we have some coffee?" Innocent nodded and Jenny took out the flask and shook it anxiously wondering if it had survived the journey.
Miraculously it was still intact and she poured two cups of strong coffee. They drank it in silence and Jenny thought

that the next two hours were going to be very long with such a silent companion as Innocent.

She had opened her mouth to say something when Innocent put his hand warningly on her arm and looked towards the opposite bank.

For a moment Jenny was unable to distinguish anything among the autumn foliage. Then she suddenly saw a glint of steel and gave a low gasp of horror when she realised that they were being watched by someone in a camouflage suit who was crouching behind a bush and training a rifle at them.

Without moving her head she scanned the undergrowth intently to see if there was anyone with him. She thought she glimpsed another body but it was difficult to tell.

Taking her cue from Innocent she made herself breathe evenly and relax while they waited to see what would happen

They must have sat there nearly ten minutes before Innocent broke the silence. "They can't be government soldiers," he said with relief in his voice, "they would have challenged us long ago if they had been."

He drew a large white handkerchief from his pocket and held it out of the window then waved it slowly to an fro. The rain had completely stopped by this time and the air was so still that Jenny hardly dared breathe.

Gradually the crouching soldier stood up and, still training his rifle towards them, took up his position in front of the bush.

Jenny had been so mesmerised by the weapon he was pointing at them that she did not notice the other soldier, also wearing camouflage, emerge from the undergrowth and stand only a few metres from them at the edge of the water.

"What is your business here?" he rasped sharply in Chakari.

To Jenny's surprise Innocent replied in Ntisi and although she was unable to follow the dialogue she felt the tension lessen. The soldier stared at her and fired questions at Innocent while Jenny hoped fervently that he believed the story.

She was surprised when he suddenly addressed her in English," So Doctor's wife, our Commissar is very sick, you must help him."

Jenny looked at Innocent.

"We must go," he said quickly taking off his shoes and rolling up his trousers.

Jenny did the same, then opened the door and gingerly let herself into the water. It came almost to her knees and she struggled through the fast-flowing stream to the waiting soldier.

He was in his early twenties but the fatigue and stress from which he was obviously suffering made him appear older. For a moment they stood looking at each other uncertainly then Innocent caught up with them and handed Jenny her rucksack. She took it gratefully and nodded approvingly when she saw that he was also carrying a large first aid kit. The young soldier led them upstream. There was no path and they had to bend double on several occasions to avoid overhanging branches. Jenny tried to make a careful note of any land-marks but the vegetation was so thick it was difficult to distinguish individual features. Once she looked back to see where they had come from but the soldier shouted at her so angrily that she did   not do it again.

After about fifteen minutes they halted in front of what appeared to be a wall of rock covered in vegetation. Their guide made a low sound like the hoot of an owl and a moment or two later a small section of the vegetation was parted to reveal the entrance to the guerrillas' hide-out. They followed the soldier into a clearing. A couple of men dressed in camouflage suits were cooking on a smokeless fire under an overhanging rock. She was dimly aware of one or two sombre figures fixing something with quiet concentration, then suddenly they were in a small cave and looking down at the inert body of a man wrapped in a blanket and lying on a bed of grass and leaves. Instinctively Jenny bent down to get a closer look at the patient. Then she gave a gasp of anguish, her head reeled and she started to tremble so violently that her teeth chattered.

The man was James.

Chapter Sixteen

For a moment the nightmare of James lying in a pool of blood and the reality were so confused that Jenny was sure that she was still dreaming.

Then suddenly a calm came over her. For the first time in months even years - she felt completely in control of the situation. Turning to the young man hovering anxiously beside her she said, "Tell me what happened."

"It happened on Saturday afternoon. The C-C-Commissar," stammered the man and stopped as he tried to gain control of himself.

Jenny nodded encouragingly and, taking James's hands in hers, started to gently massage some warmth into them. The simple action seemed to calm the soldier and he continued in halting English, "Everything was going according to plan. It was pay-day for the government workers and many of the shift workers did not bother to turn up to work. It was easy for us to take control of the radio station, the telephone exchange and the police station in both Mutape and Munari. The army had been paid at lunch-time and we knew that most of them would be so drunk that even if the Vice-President called them out immediately they would be useless. And it was true. They did not arrive in Mutape until Sunday."

Here he paused and spat on the ground. "And if our comrades in Munari had all stood by us they would not have arrived even then."

"But......?" Jenny questioned, not wanting to hurry the man but anxious to find out just what was wrong with James.

"The people in Mutape, they were pleased that the tyranny of that Funi so-called President was over," he continued passionately. "They were dancing in the streets and our Commissar was driving past and everyone was filled with joy. But," he paused and declaimed dramatically, "there was a Judas in their midst. A policeman in the crowd carried a rifle and shot him through the collar bone." Jenny looked puzzled. A wound in the shoulder did not sound very serious and yet James was lying unconscious. She put her hand to his forehead. It was burning. He gave a low moan and turned his hand restlessly and licked his parched lips.

"Did he receive treatment straight away?"

"Our Commissar is very strong," said the young soldier proudly. "He ordered the driver to continue as if nothing had happened. We used our hats to staunch the wound."

"And when did he receive treatment?" persisted Jenny.

"In the night. At our headquarters."

"You had better show me the wound." Jenny was surprised how steady her voice sounded.

As the soldier pulled back the blanket Jenny was almost overpowered from the stench coming from the wound. She swallowed hard and forced herself to look at the hole in James's right shoulder. Although it was plugged with cloth there was puss oozing out of it.

"When was this dressing last changed?" she rapped. The soldier looked shame-faced. "Last night. But we have no supplies. Our supply truck was blown up," he added his voice rising in his desperation.

"Did he receive any anti-biotics on Saturday night?"

"Yes and on Sunday morning. Our vehicle was blown up when we were - retreating - on Sunday evening."

Jenny turned to Innocent who had been standing quietly listening to the dialogue. "Let's see what we have in the first aid box," she said.

It was surprisingly well-equipped. There were even some sachets of cleaning tissues. She tore one open and cleaned her hands thoroughly while she studied the contents of the box. "I'll need boiling water," she said, "and a bag to put the old dressing in."

Her confident manner had a calming effect on the young soldier and he spoke briefly to Innocent in Ntisi. While she was waiting Jenny took James's pulse and tried not to show her alarm at the rate it was racing.

Innocent returned almost immediately with a billy can of boiling water and a plastic bag. Jenny took a pair of tweezers and dipped them in the water then proceeded to remove the soiled dressing. She was aware of her breath coming in shallow gasps as she breathed through her mouth in attempt to distance herself from the smell. "Burn it," she commanded as she dropped the stinking cloth into the bag. "And bring another one."

She wiped the tweezers with a tissue then laid them in the water for a minute in a brave attempt at sterilisation. As she did so she peered at the wound. It was a jagged hole about seven centimetres by four centimetres. She was horrified that a bullet leaving the body could cause so much damage.

James tossed his head and moaned again.

"James," said Jenny in a low voice. "James. It's Jenny. I'm going to help you."

He opened his eyes and stared at her but there was no recognition in his face. "Water," he murmured then closed his eyes again.

Jenny turned to the soldier who was looking at her in amazement and respect. Innocent too looked puzzled. "Bring some hot water for him to drink. I'll give it to him when I have renewed the dressing."

Jenny cleaned the wound as skilfully as she was able and tried hard not to flinch when James called out in pain. She sprinkled it liberally with anti-biotic powder and finally applied a fresh gauze dressing. She looked in the first aid box to see if there were any penicillin capsules but there were none. She was surprised and pleased to discover some disposable syringes containing fifteen milligrams of morphine.

"Drink this," said Jenny taking the cup of water from Innocent, "and then I'll give you something for the pain." She put her arm around James and helped him drink.

"Thank you Jenny," he said looking straight at her.

Jenny's heart leapt. He recognised her. Maybe with her help he would pull through.

James attempted to shift himself into a sitting position but sank back again. "Conrad," he said addressing the young soldier, "what news?"

Conrad coughed nervously. "They are still on reconnaissance," he replied.

Jenny thought about the other soldier waiting by the river and wondered how many more were out combing the bush.

"Tell them to report to me as soon as they return," said James his voice ringing with authority despite his condition. He licked his lips. "More water," he said to Jenny.

As she raised the cup to his mouth she felt his forehead again. it was still burning. "We must get that temperature down," she muttered desperately. She was relieved to find some soluble aspirin and she persuaded James to drink it. Then she looked at the syringe filled with morphine. She had not given an injection before and she studied the instructions. It looked quite simple. She lifted the blanket and stared at James. Should she get him to remove his trousers she wondered as she tried to fight back the shyness that threatened to overcome her. He smiled encouragingly. Quickly she plunged the needle through his trousers and into his thigh. Then she slowly pushed the plunger down and pulled the needle out.

"That should help," she said as she made James as comfortable as she could.

Then Jenny left the cave and for the first time looked at her surroundings. The ground had been swept clear of leaves but it was still wet and there was a monotonous drip of water from the trees. Instinctively she moved towards the fire and held out her hands to catch its warmth. Wordlessly one of the soldiers handed her a mug of black coffee and she perched herself on a low rock and sipped it gratefully. Now that she had finished treating James, Jenny felt out of place among the silent anxious men and she wondered what would happen next.

After a while a couple more men arrived. Their clothes were wet and they looked exhausted but they were not too tired to register surprise when they saw Jenny and Innocent. There were explanations in Ntisi and the men nodded approvingly at Jenny.

As the day wore on the weather became warmer and Jenny felt the tension lessen. When she went to look at James his breathing was more regular and he was not tossing and turning so much although his temperature was still high. Soon after noon she heard the sound of a vehicle approaching. She looked around anxiously but none of the men seemed perturbed so she assumed it was theirs. The reconnaissance party returning, she thought knowingly. The vehicle came to a halt somewhere behind the cave. Jenny strained her ears but the people inside made very little sound. She looked towards the hidden entrance that she and Innocent had come through. Then she suddenly spun round when she realised that the people had already entered the clearing.

There were five men altogether. One she recognised as the soldier with the rifle by the river. And one of the others seemed vaguely familiar. He was tall and broad-shouldered but his face was haggard and his skin sagging as if he had suddenly lost weight. He did not notice Jenny sitting quietly on the ground but turned immediately to James. The gruff voice sounded almost tender as he spoke in Ntisi and Jenny was encouraged to hear James answer in the same tongue. The man appeared to hold an important position because, after his conversation with

James he summoned the soldiers who had remained in the camp to him. He fired a rapid succession of questions at them and then strode across to where Jenny was sitting.

"So we meet again," he said extending his hand as Jenny stood up and looked at him in bewilderment. "I don't know how you come to be travelling in this direction but they tell me you are trying to save the Commissar." He paused, "You do recognise me?"

"Yes," said Jenny as comprehension dawned upon her, "you're Leintu."

"Is the land-rover yours?" he asked.

Jenny shook her head and said nothing.

"Who does it belong to?" asked Leintu impatiently.

"George Farrier."

Leintu looked around sharply. "Where is he?"

"He's at his farm near Fort Joan," said Jenny wearily. "I'm trying to get back to my husband and children."

"In this direction?" Leintu snorted disbelievingly.

"All the main roads are blocked. Innocent said he would drive me as far as Yonda or even Mutape via the small roads."

"Do you have supplies in your vehicle?"

Jenny was surprised when Innocent answered that they did.

"Good. Your driver will go with one of my men and fetch it as soon as the water level has receded. In fact it may be possible to drive it out now."

Leintu issued a few instructions in Ntisi and Innocent and one of the soldiers departed. He continued speaking in Ntisi to the remaining soldiers and Jenny, feeling herself dismissed, went to look at James.

He opened his eyes as she approached, they were very bright and she thought for a moment that he was recovering. Then he started to speak - disjointed words in several different languages - and Jenny realised that the glitter in his eyes was due to his delirium.

There must be something more we can do, she thought desperately as she took his cold hand in hers. She thought that he would feel more comfortable if she washed his hands and face so she got up and brought some water from the fire. She took a face cloth, soap and towel from her rucksack and then carefully washed his hands, face and neck in the warm water. She dried them thoroughly and continued to rub his hands until they became warm. Then, for want of anything else to do, she checked his pulse again and was gratified when he opened his eyes and murmured, "Thank you Jenny."

Jenny was dimly aware of the shadows lengthening as she sat by her friend willing him to recover. She heard George's land-rover and watched Innocent and a soldier come into the clearing with a box of provisions and some blankets. There was a flurry of activity around the camp fire and sometime later Jenny was handed a steaming plate of stew.

"Will the Commissar eat anything?" asked Conrad, hovering anxiously.

"He might manage a little gravy when he wakes up," said Jenny.

She ate her food hungrily suddenly realising that it was the first meal she had had since supper the night before. With George, she thought in a sudden wave of longing. She looked upwards forcing herself not to think back and watched a vulture gliding in a circle above the camp. She shivered and stood up.

The movement must have disturbed James for he woke and sat up.

"That smells good," he said clearly.

Jenny gave a gasp of surprise and delight. "Conrad, bring the Commissar some gravy," she ordered.

At the sound of James's voice Leintu hurried over with a questioning grin on his face. "That's right comrade, you'll soon be better," he said eagerly and when Conrad brought the mug of gravy he gave it to him himself.

James took a couple of sips then asked again "What news?"

"There are ten of us here but we have no contact with any of the others."

"And what of the government forces?"

"We sighted some earlier further west travelling towards Fort Joan."

James nodded, his intelligent eyes now quite alert. "Then we must move north and across the Van as soon as possible. What vehicles do we have?"

"Just the armoured patrol car. Conrad and his crew had to abandon their vehicle and get here on foot." He paused then added, "They lost Nkpe on the way."

James made no comment although the sudden anger on his face showed that he had understood.

Jenny wondered how ten men including James in his condition were going to escape in one small patrol car. Leintu was obviously thinking the same. "We'll have to commandeer the land-rover," he said abruptly.

James looked hard at Jenny. "Where are you heading for?"

"Yonda," whispered Jenny.

"See that she gets there," said James sharply to Leintu. Then he sank down and drifted off to sleep.

Darkness had fallen and Jenny shivered in the cool air.

"Your driver thought you might run into trouble and he came well supplied," said Leintu handing Jenny a blanket and putting another one over James.

Jenny sat huddled near James wondering what was going to happen. She saw Leintu talking to Innocent and a moment later Innocent came over to her.

He was in an agitated state and for a moment he just stood in front of her cracking his knuckles.

"What's the matter?" asked Jenny.

Innocent swallowed hard then said, "They say it is too dangerous to take you to Yonda. They say they must drop you at the edge of the mountains and you must walk." Jenny said nothing then, as if she had not heard said, "And what about you?"

"When I have driven you as near as Yonda as possible I come back here for the others then we take two vehicles to the river. As long as there has been no," he paused and licked his lips, "trouble, I can return home then."

"What will stop us from just driving on to Yonda?" Innocent looked surprised at the naivety of the question. "There will be a soldier escorting us to make sure we don't."

Jenny shook her head slowly trying to take in the implications of what Innocent was telling her. "When are we expected to leave?" she asked keeping her voice as steady as she could.

"Early tomorrow morning I suppose. They can't expect you to walk in the dark," said Innocent angrily.

"I hope James has recovered sufficiently to travel by then," said Jenny looking with compassion at the sleeping figure.

"You should try and get some sleep yourself," said Innocent gruffly and then walked away.

Using the rucksack for a pillow, Jenny made herself as comfortable as she could on the hard ground and fell asleep almost immediately.

When she awoke a few hours later she thought in panic that she was back in her aunt's house where she had been so unhappy after the death of her father. The house backed on to a railway line and she had sometimes been kept awake by the shunting of trains. The noise that she could hear now reminded her of those far-off trains. Jenny strained her ears but could not hear a vehicle. She was aware of the broad figure of Leintu bending over James and then she realised what the sound was. It was James breathing - or attempting to breathe. The breaths came in slow gasps and seemed to rattle around his chest. The death rattle, thought Jenny in terror as she too struggled for breath. She looked at Leintu and saw the desperation in his eyes as he fumbled for his friend's pulse. She lifted his wrist and for a moment was relieved to feel the pulse beating normally. Then she wondered if her fingers had slipped for it stopped for several seconds, then she felt it again faster. There seemed nothing to say or do, she just sat feeling the pulse become more and more irregular.

How many minutes or hours passed Jenny had no idea but suddenly she was aware of a subtle change. The stertorous breathing ceased and James spoke in his normal voice to Leintu. Jenny did not understand what he said because it was in their own language but it seemed as if James was giving Leintu instructions and encouragement.

Then he turned to Jenny. "How is Darren?" he said.

"He's well." And she knew he was. And that David and Richard were safe and well also.

"Good. Tell him - tell him that sometimes the chameleon does not change its colour quickly enough."

They were only just able to catch what he said then he sank back and Jenny felt his pulse become weaker and weaker until she could feel it no longer.

They continued to sit by their friend, neither wanting to admit that the end had finally come.

Jenny was surprised to see tears streaming down Leintu's cheeks and his shoulders shaking in a silent paroxysm of grief.

She herself felt nothing at all. Just cold and hard and empty.

Gradually Leintu gained control of himself, leant over and closed James's eyes and then walked heavily into the clearing. With the exception of Conrad the men were sleeping soundly, exhausted after the ordeals they had suffered. Leintu seemed loathe to disturb them and he squatted down by Conrad. Jenny saw the distraught young soldier jump to his feet, throw back his head and open his mouth to make the traditional wailing sound that announces a person's death. Quick as a flash Leintu clapped his hand over Conrad's mouth to stop him from making the blood-curdling cry that would announce their whereabouts for miles around.

He went and awoke Innocent then walked over to Jenny who was still sitting motionless beside the body that had so recently been her friend as well as leader of the rebel forces.

"It's one thirty-three," he said consulting his digital watch. "Get yourself some coffee and be ready to leave in half an hour."

Jenny joined Innocent who was already busy by the fire. Gradually the rest of the men awoke and their grief hung about heavily as they learned of the death of their Commissar.

After a while a taciturn soldier whose name Jenny had been unable to catch came and spoke roughly to Innocent.

"We must go," he said to Jenny draining his mug of coffee. The three of them went to Leintu who issued some last-minute instructions in Ntisi. Innocent tried to argue but Leintu spoke angrily and, glancing uneasily at Jenny, Innocent nodded.

"You will deliver a message to inform our people of his death. Innocent will tell you where to go and what to say." Leintu held out his hand. "Goodbye Jenny North. You made his death easier. Go well."

Jenny and Innocent followed the soldier out of the camp to where George's land-rover was hidden. Innocent got into the driver's seat and Jenny climbed in and sat down between the two men.

They drove slowly, not using lights, and it was nearly half an hour later before they joined the track that she and Innocent had been about to travel on the day before.

Innocent needed all his concentration to drive in the dark and although she was anxious to know where she was going to be left and how she was to find James's people, she asked no questions. Despite the bumps she managed to doze for an hour but it was still dark when she awoke. She wondered if they would reach their destination, but the feeling of urgency that she had felt the day before had left her. She knew now that it was James who had needed her. And she had been too late.

She re-lived every detail of the previous day wondering what she could have done to have saved him. If only there had been some penicillin in the first aid kit. But then it might just have given rise to more false hopes. She knew that once septicaemia had taken hold it was difficult to combat, even in normal conditions. But was there nothing else she could have done she wondered guiltily.

She closed her eyes again and an image of Richard appeared pacing distractedly in their sitting room in England. He had just returned from the hospital with the news that Bill was being discharged and would never walk again. She had tried to console him when he blamed himself for being unable to cure his brother. She had found it hard to understand why he had felt it was his fault when he had obviously done everything he could for Bill. But then Sheila and his mother had felt that the hospital and therefore Richard should have found a miracle cure. And, unable to bear the burden of his failure, he had unconsciously tried to be the doctor who, not only never made any mistakes, but also was always available to any sick person who needed him.

Did she really want to go back to him she asked herself wearily. Anyway, it didn't matter, she was going back to Bambo and on the way she had to deliver a message for James. She was very tired and would just take one step at a time.

As they travelled east the sky began to lighten but it was still dark when the soldier ordered Innocent to pull off the road and park half under a large thorn bush. They all got out of the driver's side and then followed the soldier through the bush for about five minutes until they came to a huge baobab tree. Jenny was so pleased to have the opportunity to stretch her legs that she felt no fear of what might happen next.

She watched with interest as the soldier unwound a rope from around his waist. The massive trunk of the baobab rose for about four metres before dividing into two great branches. The soldier threw the rope over the lower of the branches, handed the end to Innocent then, with remarkable agility, proceeded to climb up the trunk..

When he reached the cleft of the tree he pulled up the rope and then, feeling around the tree, he produced a large iron hook. Jenny watched with fascination as he attached the hook to the end of the rope and then let it down into the trunk of the tree.

"It's hollow inside," said Innocent in explanation.

The soldier shone a torch into the tree to see what he was doing. There was a clanking as the hook struck metal then the soldier pulled on the rope and brought out a jerry can. He swung the rope down the outside of the trunk, Innocent took off the jerry can then the soldier pulled the rope up again. He brought up four more jerry cans before climbing down to Jenny and Innocent.

The soldier picked up two of the cans and with a curt nod at the others he started to walk back to the land-rover. Innocent glowered at him as he picked up two cans and watched Jenny struggle with the fifth. They made slow progress as Jenny was forced to keep stopping to transfer the jerry can from one hand to the other. Her palms were red and numb by the time she thankfully put it down for the last time next to the land-rover.

"Come!" ordered the soldier when all the jerry cans were loaded.

"No," said Innocent firmly. "We are nearly at our destination and Jenny must have some refreshment before she leaves us."

He took the flask which he had filled before they left and poured out three cups of strong sweet coffee. As they drank Innocent told Jenny in a low voice what she must do. It sounded quite straightforward, the house that she had to visit was on the edge of Yonda near the mountains. Innocent assured her that the track that she must take was quite well-defined and in any case all she had to do was to travel due east which was easy at that time of day.

"But what if I meet a military patrol?" Jenny could not help asking.

"Tell them that you were captured by the rebels, they stole your vehicle but you managed to escape. Act very confused and beg for their protection."

"It won't be difficult to act confused," said Jenny drily. "But I sincerely hope I don't run into trouble."

The soldier coughed impatiently.

"We must go," said Innocent. "We want to be well away from here before sunrise."

They got back into the land-rover and Innocent drove recklessly along the track. It was becoming lighter all the time and the three of them were becoming increasingly nervous.

Ten minutes passed then Innocent left the track again and drove between the bushes cracking branches as he went. Then he suddenly halted and got out, holding the door open for Jenny.

"This is it," he said, his voice a mixture of apology and relief.

Jenny looked around fearfully. About five hundred metres ahead the ground rose steeply.

"Once you are on top of the ridge you will see a path winding down to the town. It is a bit exposed in places but with luck you shouldn't be seen from a distance." Innocent looked critically at her jeans and brown jumper. "you are quite well camouflaged apart from your face. Keep that jumper on even if you get hot, it's a good colour."

Jenny bent down and picked up a handful of soil which she rubbed into her face and Innocent nodded approvingly.

The land-rover engine was still running and the soldier inside moved impatiently.

Innocent held out his hand. "Goodbye Jenny. May God be with you."

"And with you," she replied.

Then she stood stock-still as she watched Innocent get back into the vehicle and drive off in the direction they had come from.

Would they make it in time she wondered. And would George get his land-rover back?

Trying to throw off such thoughts she turned and started to walk towards the ridge.

Chapter Seventeen

Jenny has reached the top of the mountain and a gentle wind is blowing in her face. She is walking along a well-defined path at the edge of the ridge. The solitude is overwhelming. From a long way away she hears a bleat. She stands motionless, not knowing if she is in the real world or a waking dream. A shadow passes over her and she looks up, every muscle taut with fear. For an instant she sees David playing in the garden. Then she gives a silent scream as a bird flies out in front of her. She feels as if she is falling but she remains standing stiffly unable to move.

Jenny forced herself to look at the bird resting on the branch of a bush.

The dove cooed and cocked its head encouragingly at her. She was still panting after her scramble up the rocky slope but as she stood watching the bird her breathing became steady. She looked east and saw the Van plain stretching out to the horizon and every now and again caught a glint of the river. The ridge fell down steeply to the plain and immediately below she could see a jumble of thatched and corrugated tin roofs of the small town of Yonda.

Just ahead the path turned sharply to the right and went down the side of the ridge. The sun had risen but the air was still cool and Jenny continued walking at a brisk pace. All her senses were alert as she kept a sharp lookout for soldiers and also for natural hazards such as snakes.

Once she heard voices and dived into some bushes at the side of the path and waited, her heart beating violently. A few minutes later an old man and a woman carrying a basket on her head passed close by. As Jenny crouched waiting for them to pass out of earshot she noticed some pretty pink, blue and white flowers. Some were growing close to the ground with tiny petals and others were on longer stems waving in the breeze. Without really realising what she was doing Jenny picked one of each kind, four in all, and wrapped them carefully in her handkerchief then put them in the outside pocket of her rucksack. She waited a few minutes more and then continued on her way.

Half an hour later she was standing at a fork in the path at the bottom of the ridge. She stood for a moment as she recalled Innocent's instructions. The right hand path led directly to the town but the left hand veered away from it. She hesitated for a moment then confidently took the left hand path.

It was nearly two hours since Innocent and the soldier had dropped her. She wondered if they were back at the camp: they might be as they could drive faster in the day light. She wondered if bringing her had caused them much delay, but they had obviously needed to get to the fuel cache anyway.

As Jenny walked she could hear the tinkle of cow bells and the occasional cock crow. Smoke from people's breakfast fires drifted upwards and the scents of porridge, hot fat and cow dung mingled together in the fresh breeze. The thought that the President of the country had been shot only five days previously and that fierce fighting had been continuing since then seemed utterly ridiculous in that tranquil atmosphere.

Jenny felt bowed down with sadness as she thought about the lives that had been wasted. And she wondered how she would summon the courage to bring the news of James's death to his people.

She passed a couple of traditional compounds and came to a halt by a small shop. "A packet of biscuits please," she said to the girl behind the counter. She fumbled with her change, playing for time. She had been told to speak to Mr. Matisa, a white-haired old man with a scar on his cheek, or to his son. She had paid the girl and was wondering what to do when a man of about forty entered the shop from the back.

"Good morning," said Jenny uncertainly in Chakari. "I am Jenny North from Bambo. I am a stranger here."

The man extended his hand and looked at her quizzically as he introduced himself as Daniel Matisa.

Jenny gave a sigh of relief then, with a wary look at the girl behind the counter, said, "Is there anywhere I can wash my hands? I fell and cut myself as I was coming here."

"Come this way," said the man gravely leading Jenny out through the door at the back.

"I have a message for you," she said in a low voice as they walked towards a well in the courtyard.

The man looked at her keenly taking in her dishevelled appearance and dirt-stained face. He walked past the well and Jenny followed him into a dimly-lit hut.

Lying on a skin mat on the floor was an elderly man with white hair and a scar on one cheek. When he saw Jenny he sat up and spoke to his son fearfully in Ntisi.

Daniel Matisa shook his head and indicated to Jenny that she should sit. The chair was rickety and the back sloped away uncomfortably so Jenny perched on the edge, glad at least to take the weight off her feet.

"Who sent you?" he asked after a short silence.

"Leintu."

"And what news do you bring from my cousin?"

Jenny lowered her eyes. "Bad news," she whispered. "James is dead."

The old man gave a gasp but his son silenced him.

"That is bad news indeed," said Daniel. "He is my first cousin and my father's favourite nephew. He was highly regarded in the family. His parents will.....," he stopped and brushed his hand over his eyes. "Tell me all you know," he continued trying to keep his voice steady.

So Jenny recounted all that had happened in the last twenty four hours. It took a long time because Daniel kept translating for his father. They wanted to know exactly who was left and, although Jenny did not know all their names, she managed to describe them to their satisfaction. When she had finished Daniel said, "And how do you plan to get to Bambo? It is dangerous for you to stay here." When Jenny mentioned George's friend the vet he shook his head sadly. He said that he knew the vet well because his daughter worked for him. But he had left for Mutape the Friday of the coup and had not yet returned.

"You see, it is forbidden to travel on the main roads. They are closed to all except police and army vehicles."

Jenny sighed. Despite the two men in the hut she felt utterly alone. And she knew that if she was discovered with Ntisi sympathisers her chances of getting back to Bambo in the near future were slim.

The silence hung heavily in the darkened hut as each of the three were absorbed in their sombre thoughts. Jenny thought back to Innocent's advice as to what she should do if she ran into a patrol. She had had very little to do with the police in Chark and nothing at all with the military so she had no idea what their attitude would be to a white woman travelling alone when the country was in a state of emergency. If there was someone she could turn to for advice. But the Charkian whose opinion she had valued most was dead, buried by now in an unmarked grave somewhere in the mountains. She thought back to his last words - "Tell him that sometimes the chameleon does not change colour quickly enough." That had been such a carefree day together at Amos's farm.

Jenny started. Thinking of Amos jogged her memory. Sue and Larry had stayed with his brother when they travelled north the Christmas before last. She cleared her throat. "Is Mr. Bambo still the Commandant of the police station?"

Daniel looked surprised. "Why yes. Do you know him?"

Jenny explained that she knew his brother and she wondered if she went to the police station and said that her truck had been taken by the rebels it might help.

Daniel looked anxious. "You must do what you feel is right. But you must not to let them bully you into telling them their whereabouts."

"No, I'll be careful."

"Would you like some tea before you go? And a wash?" Daniel smiled politely but Jenny could see that he was anxious for her to be gone.

She stood up and shook hands with the old man. As she turned towards the door of the hut she was dazzled by the sun and did not notice how low the door-way was. She started to stride out purposefully and hit her forehead smack against the door-frame.

Jenny reeled in pain. Daniel caught her arm and led her back to the chair. She felt blood trickling down her face but when she dabbed the wound with a tissue she was relieved to find that it was only a small cut. I'll have a black eye to show for my experience if nothing else she thought ruefully. Daniel offered to get water to bathe her forehead and she was just about to thank him when the thought of the black eye changed her mind. She thought that it was just possible she might excite some sympathy from the police if she walked in as she was.

She stood up, anxious to be on her way, but faintness threatened to overcome her and she was forced to sit down again. Daniel and his father looked at her anxiously as she took her water bottle from her rucksack, had a few sips and then opened the packet of biscuits she had bought. The water was tepid and the biscuits dry crackers but they revived her and when she stood up again the faintness had gone.

"Don't come outside with me," she said. "Just tell me the way to the police station."

The old man muttered something to his son and looked at Jenny with distrust.

She bent down and clasped his hands. "I won't betray you," she said and added almost inaudibly, "I too loved your nephew."

The old man smiled for the first time. "God be with you," he said in halting English.

"And with you."

She looked at Daniel and he stood beside her in the doorway and gave clear instructions how to get to the police station.

Once again they shook hands and Jenny walked slowly but steadily out of the compound.

Without a backward glance she continued walking along the road by which she had come. The houses became more concentrated and she passed several people also walking or standing chatting. They greeted her politely, as was the custom and although several of them stared at her they let her pass on her way.

When she sighted a flag pole ahead of her she knew that she must be approaching the police station. The Charkian flag fluttered forlornly at half-mast and her spirits sank partly in trepidation for herself and partly in sorrow for the people of Chark.

Her pace became slower and it was with a great effort that she forced herself to keep going until she came to the gate of the police station. Usually they were flung open but now they were closed and a soldier and a policeman, both armed, stood to attention behind them.

Jenny approached slowly and greeted them in Chakari. The policeman reluctantly replied but the soldier said nothing although Jenny could feel him looking at her and was fearfully aware of the loaded rifle he was holding. Continuing in halting Chakari she asked if she could see Mr. Bambo the station Commandant. The policeman looked surprised but did not appear any friendlier. He conferred with the soldier in a low voice and then turned around and marched officiously into the police station. He came back five minutes later, opened the gate and curtly told Jenny to follow him.

The walk across the dusty parade ground to the police buildings seemed endless to Jenny. Her head throbbed and she was uncomfortably hot in her brown jumper.

When they reached the enquiry desk the policeman left her and returned to his gate duty. Jenny stood waiting for the constable behind the counter to stop writing and address her.

"Yes?" he rasped after Jenny was beginning to wonder if he would ever look up.

"I would like to see the Commandant, Inspector Bambo." The constable scowled. "Our Commandant is very busy. What is your business with him?"

Jenny swallowed. "I wish to speak to him personally."

"He is busy," said the constable dismissively and started to shuffle papers.

Jenny waited a moment or two then, plucking up courage said, "Please will you tell him that I am from Bambo."

He looked at her with increasing hostility and said coldly, "In Chark we do not favour people just because we are from the same home-town."

Jenny drew in a breath and cursed herself inwardly. She felt totally exhausted and leant against the counter wondering how she could get past the officious young constable in front of her. He took absolutely no notice of her although from the way he fidgeted with the papers in front of him he seemed uncomfortably aware of her presence.

It was a relief to both of them when the telephone rang. The constable answered it then opened the door behind him. Thank goodness thought Jenny, he's calling someone, maybe I'll be able to speak to them as well. But to her disappointment the constable conducted the conversation from where he was and then returned to the phone. He left the door open and Jenny saw that it was a large room and there appeared to be several people in it. She leant over the counter and coughed in an attempt to attract their attention. "Silence!" hissed the constable putting his hand over the mouth of the receiver. He finished his conversation and started to close the door. Jenny leant forward in a last attempt to attract attention - and fainted.

When she came round a few minutes later she was sitting on a hard chair in a small room. A policewoman was standing looking at her while a policeman was sorting through some things at a desk. When Jenny looked more closely she saw that it was the contents of her rucksack. "Are you alright?" asked the policewoman dispassionately. "Can I have some water please?"

The woman nodded and opened the door then called to someone on the other side to bring water.

Jenny watched, her eyes smouldering with anger, as the policeman examined every item of hers in detail.

Although she had nothing to hide she felt violated and she found it hard to remain silent although she knew it was essential that she stay calm.

She was relieved when someone arrived with a mug of water; her mouth felt dry and the liquid helped a little.

The last item that the policeman took from her rucksack was the rose that Winston had picked for her, carefully wrapped in a tissue. As Jenny watched him look at it and then at Jenny with incomprehension she wanted to scream "That's mine!" but she remained silent. Finally the policeman put his hand into the outside pocket and drew out Jenny's handkerchief. Inside were the flowers, already beginning to wilt.

Once again he gave Jenny a puzzled look but the hostility that Jenny had felt as she first came round was gone. The innocuous collection of items on the table, mainly clothing, seemed to show that Jenny did not constitute a threat to the country's security.

"What is your business here?" he asked sternly but politely.

"I came to ask for help. I am trying to reach my family in Bambo but I was captured by - the guerrillas." Jenny choked on the last word and the policeman waited patiently until she had drunk some more water.

"How were you travelling?"

"By land-rover." Jenny drew in a deep breath, determined not to choke again. "They took my vehicle and left me to find my way as best I could."

There was a murmur of sympathy and the two police officers conferred in Chakari. Then the man stood up and left the room.

"He is going to report to Inspector Bambo," said the policewoman. She looked at the congealed blood on Jenny's dirt-stained face.

"I think they gave you a bad time." She lowered her voice and leant closer, her face now full of pity. "Did they rape you as well?"

"No," said Jenny with icy calm. "They were only interested in my vehicle."

They waited in silence till the policeman returned.

"The Inspector will see you now," he said and indicated that Jenny should follow him.

Despite his immaculate blue uniform the man sitting behind the desk looked so much like Amos that Jenny nearly cried with relief.

He greeted her sternly but not unkindly and dismissed the subordinate officer.

"Now tell me exactly who you are and what you are doing here," he said sitting back in his chair with his hands resting lightly against his paunch.

Jenny took a breath and in a clear confident voice said, "I am Jenny North. My husband is a doctor at William

Banks Hospital. Our friend in Fort Joan invited me to spend a few days holiday with him as I hadn't had the opportunity to travel much in Chark and we are probably returning to England in September. He picked me up last Friday and the plan was that I returned yesterday. But of course the government had forbidden people to use the main roads. I got terribly worried about my children. I wondered what they would think when I didn't return. They are only four and six, you see they wouldn't understand. Also I thought that my husband might be very busy if there were many casualties after the coup and he wouldn't have time to look after them. My friend tried to persuade me to wait but I wouldn't listen." Jenny put her hand to her forehead which had started to throb again. "I wish I had," she said and at that point she almost meant it.
"Do you mean you drove through the mountains alone?" the Inspector was more incredulous than suspicious.
"Yes. I kept to the main road so it wasn't too difficult although I knew I was breaking the law."
"But we had vehicles patrolling that road all the time." Jenny bit her lip but continued smoothly, "I'd only been going about an hour when the guerrillas picked me up." The lie seemed to satisfy him. "What happened then?"
"They blindfolded me and made me sit in the back of the vehicle."
"When did this happen?"
"Yesterday morning."
"And where have you been since?"
"I spent most of yesterday in the vehicle. They kept stopping. Once they were stopped for a long time and then put some guns - arms - in the back." Jenny shivered when she realised what her journey might have been like.
"Have you no idea where you were at this point?"
"No. I'm sorry."
"Did you not hear anything they said?"

Jenny shook her head. "They were speaking in a foreign language."

"What sort of language?" The Inspector's voice was sharp.

"An, an African language," stammered Jenny.

"Ah." The Inspector relaxed and muttered to himself, "Ntisi. And then what happened?"

Jenny continued slowly, "It was dark by the time they let me get out. I was kept blindfolded so I don't know where I was."

"Was it a hide-out?"

"I suppose so."

"How many people were there?"

"It was difficult to tell," said Jenny cagily.

"You must have heard voices, about how many do you think?"

Jenny could see why the Matisas had been so anxious about her going to the police.

"Well," she said, "I wouldn't like to swear that it's the truth, but probably about half a dozen."

"Are you sure there weren't more?"

"I don't know. I was frightened. Sometimes it felt like a hundred."

"Alright. Now if there were only a few you must have heard some names mentioned."

Jenny considered for a moment. He was right. What should she say?

"I think there was someone called Thomas," she said at last.

The Inspector reached forward for a pen and wrote down the name. "And who else?"

Jenny began to quake. She had never been very good at lying. I'll have to tell him the truth she thought wildly. She licked her lips then realised that she could tell part of the truth.

"They mentioned someone called Nkpe," she said.

"Was he there?"

"I don't think so. They seemed to be talking about him."

"And was anyone else mentioned?"

Jenny shook her head. "I really don't know. They didn't give me anything to eat and I kept drifting to sleep."

The Inspector accepted that then looking at her straight in the eyes asked, "Did you hear the name Matisa?"

Jenny considered for a moment then shook her head again. "No, I didn't hear that name."

"Alright. Now how did you get here?"

"They left just before sunrise. I thought they had left me completely alone but one man stopped behind to untie my blindfold. He told me to wait until sunrise and then walk due east and I would reach Yonda. And that's what I did."

"What did the man look like?"

"He was wearing a camouflage suit. He was tall and young but he didn't have any distinctive features."

Inspector Bambo sat looking at Jenny for a moment or two. Finally he said, "Alright Mrs. North, I believe your story. And I will help you return to your family." He picked up the telephone and issued some instructions. "P.C. Angelina will see that you have a wash and something to eat while I decide what we are to do next."

"Thank you Inspector," said Jenny hardly daring to breathe.

Chapter Eighteen

Two hours later Jenny was sitting in the back of a police land-cruiser heading for Mutape. She was not blindfolded but it was uncomfortable and she was very thankful that her story had not been true. On the floor beside her lay her rucksack - a couple of kilos heavier because of the oranges the Inspector had asked her to take to his brother.

There were two other passengers who had been stranded in Yonda due to the coup. Jenny greeted them politely at the beginning of the journey but was too exhausted to talk or even take anything in.

It was not until they neared the outskirts of Mutape that Jenny began to take an interest in her surroundings. She could see oil rigs rising ominously from the plain in the setting sun. She glared at them angrily as she inwardly blamed them for causing her friend's death. Then she attempted to pull herself together as she realised that the unequal distribution of the oil revenue was a symptom, not a cause, of a situation rooted in the colonial and pre-colonial past.

They stopped at a road block and Jenny and the other passengers were obliged to show the paper they had been issued at Yonda police station which gave them permission to travel.

When they continued she looked about to see what Mutape was like and what damage had been done. But they skirted the city centre and came to a stop at the railway station.

A policeman got out of the cab and told Jenny that she had reached her destination. He said that the passenger train to Munari was due to arrive sometime that evening. Jenny thanked him, picked up her rucksack, briskly said goodbye to her fellow travellers and got out of the land-cruiser. There were lots of people milling about but not in the loud almost frenetic manner of crowds at a railway station.

They had wary expressions and many of them looked tired as if they had spent several days waiting for the train. Jenny joined the queue at the ticket office and waited patiently for almost an hour until she reached the booking clerk. She bought a first class ticket which entitled her to a sleeper and then joined the queue of people waiting on the platform. It was dark by this time and the air was chilly. As she moved slowly towards the platform gate she looked forward to the luxury of travelling in a first class sleeper. Once trough the gate it was another hour before the train arrived and Jenny joined the other passengers sitting quietly on the ground. A young man sat beside her and tried to engage her in conversation but she replied in monosyllables until he gave up and wandered away.

A scuffle broke out among some passengers waiting further along the platform but it was quickly stopped by a couple of the dozen or so policemen who were vigilantly patrolling the station.

Suddenly there was a hoot and the train appeared and at the same time pandemonium broke loose among the crowd. Jenny scrambled up and put her rucksack on her back then remained absolutely still as people shoved and pushed as they all tried to board the train at once.

She waited for a while then pushed her way along the platform until she came to the compartment she had been allocated. There were four bunks in the compartment - two either side - and two young Charkian women were already sitting on one of the bottom bunks. Jenny greeted them and threw her rucksack on to a top bunk. A few minutes later another white woman appeared. She was younger than Jenny and had the look of a seasonal hitch-hiker.

"Going far?" she asked giving a general nod.

"Munari," replied one of the women.

"Do you live there?" the question had an inquisitiveness that Jenny did not like and after a few more questions it became evident that she was angling for accommodation. Jenny was determined to keep her destination unknown if possible.

She was surprised when the door opened and a Charkian woman with two small children came in. Everyone checked their tickets and found that they had all been allocated the same compartment.

"The conductor will sort it out once we're off," said the white girl knowledgeably.

Just as the whistle blew and the train started the door opened again and a huge woman wearing the distinctive coloured wrapper and turban from Tambalia suddenly filled the compartment. She dropped her luggage on the floor and sat down heavily next to the children, panting and mopping her forehead.

The white girl winked at Jenny and scrambled on to the top bunk. Jenny felt like doing the same but did not feel like talking to the girl so she remained where she was.

The two children sitting quietly opposite her were about the same ages as Darren and David. Jenny smiled at them and they smiled shyly back. She felt a sudden pang and a piercing pain in her chest. It was because of her fear for their safety that she had undertaken this crazy journey. Her anguish at James's death and her fear of being turned in as an accomplice to the rebels had made her forget everything else but now that she was sitting so close to these children she felt their vulnerability and dependence on their mother and knew that Darren and David were also vulnerable and dependent on her.

The train rattled over a bridge. What had happened to them? Were they in danger? Jenny shuddered and clasped her hands tightly in her lap as she told herself that in twelve hours she would know.

When the conductor appeared Jenny did not take part in the arguing. It was pointless anyway as the train was obviously carrying more passengers than it should be. In the end she and the white girl shared one top bunk, the two young women the other, the mother and her children had a bottom bunk and the large Tambalian lady had a bunk to herself.

The hitch-hiker tried to get people to talk about the coup but everyone was either too tired or reluctant to talk and finally they all drifted off to sleep.

Jenny slept fitfully as the train rumbled and clattered through the night, stopping at numerous halts and small stations.

A loud rap at the door made her sit up with a start then she looked down with relief as she heard the conductor call "Morning coffee!" and enter with a tray of cups and coffee pots. The two children stayed asleep but everyone else looked sleepily for their money and took the coffee gladly after the cramped night they had spent.

Jenny looked at her watch. It was seven o'clock. She wondered what time they would reach Bambo. She decided to have a wash and ask the conductor on the way back.

There was a queue at the toilets and they weren't very clean. Jenny gave her face a quick wipe and noticed that her forehead was still swollen and was beginning to turn blue.

She found the conductor and he said they were due to reach Bambo at eight o'clock. Once again Jenny felt a surge of apprehension. Were the boys alright? And even if they were, what would they say when they saw her? And what would Richard say?

She did not want to return to the crowded compartment so she stayed in the corridor and tried to keep her mind occupied by sorting through her rucksack.

"Looking for something?" asked a friendly American voice.

"Just for a bit of peace and quiet," replied Jenny coldly.

"Sorry I asked," said the voice.

Jenny picked up her address book and flicked through it. There was only one entry under 'F' and that was a recent one. Maria's address was carefully printed in George's steady hand. Jenny looked at it for a moment before letting it drop back into her rucksack. She had a sudden longing to be back at Rossano with George, to wake up in his bed and find that the last two days had been a dream. But her dreams had caused enough trouble already. Resolutely she put on her rucksack and stood gazing unseeing out of the window. Suddenly the countryside appeared familiar. The railway ran parallel to the Mutape-Munari road and ahead of her on the eastern side of the track lay Bambo. Then they veered away from the main road and crossed the mix of bush and small farms on the edge of the village. Jenny made her way to the door at the end of the corridor and pulled down the window. She felt strangely elated as she leant out of the window and looked at the familiar sights. She glanced upwards at the hospital built on the hillside. Was it home? She didn't know, but at least for the moment it was the end of her journey.

The train wheezed into the station, there was a grinding of brakes and the train stopped.

Without a backward glance Jenny leapt nimbly down the steps and strode along the small platform. She handed her ticket to the collector and, with a confidence she had not felt for years, she walked across the station yard and took one of the tracks that wound between the compounds on its leisurely way through the town.

It took almost an hour to reach the hospital gates as the path led uphill the whole way. Her sense of elation receded as she became warm and weary but she still retained the quiet confidence in herself that had been growing since her night in the rebel's hide-out.

She hesitated as she approached the tree where only a week ago George had been waiting for her, but she hurried on.

Jonah was sitting in his usual position at the hospital gates. Jenny made herself stop to greet him civilly. She looked him straight in the eye and saw him as an old and feeble man - and not the malevolent kidnapper of her fantasy. Nevertheless she quickened her pace in her anxiety to be with her sons again and she was almost running by the time she reached the garden gate. She paused for a moment outside, then drew a breath and opened the gate, closing it quietly behind her.

Darren and David were kneeling on the veranda by a large bowl of soapy water. They each had a piece of plastic pipe that looked as if it had once been part of a hospital drip and they were totally absorbed in blowing bubbles.

Darren blew a bubble that was bigger than the rest and it floated across the grass towards Jenny. They shouted gleefully and ran towards it.

As the bubble reached Jenny it burst and the boys looked at her in amazement and awe.

"Hello," she said bending down and giving them each a kiss. "Are you alright?"

"Oh yes," said Darren airily. "Daddy brought us these from the hospital and we're the best bubble-makers in the world."

"Where is Daddy?"

"He's at work." Darren tugged at his mother's hand. "Let me show you how big I can blow bubbles."

David took her other hand and Jenny allowed herself to have the delights of bubble-making explained to her.

She sat on the verandah feeling slightly dizzy after her walk from the station and realised that she had had very little to eat or drink in the last forty-eight hours.

She was wondering whether to go inside and make herself a cup of coffee when the gate clicked. She looked up and saw Richard hurrying towards her.

"Jenny!" he said and stopped just in front of her his face a mixture of joy, anger, bewilderment and concern.

"Yes, I'm back," she said trying to fight back the dizziness.
"But are you alright?" Richard's doctor's eyes anxiously
took in the lump on her forehead, the dark rings under her
eyes and the tautness of the mouth caused by suffering.
"I've got a lot to tell you. But - yes - I'm alright. And
you?"
"We're alright aren't we boys?"
He brushed his hand through his hair then, hardly
conscious of what he was doing, took off his glasses and
peered at Jenny.
"Yes, we've been alright - haven't we boys?" he repeated,
his agitated manner belying his words.
He continued to stare awkwardly at the dishevelled
stranger standing motionless before him. Despite her
appearance Jenny carried with her a pride and self-
containment which at that moment seemed impenetrable.
Richard held out his hand towards her then let it fall.
He looked at the rucksack still on her back and his face
was drawn with anguish.
"You are - back?" he said fighting to gain his accustomed
self-control.
Jenny nodded but felt suddenly too weary to say any more.
Relief made Richard's voice sharp. "You look exhausted,"
he rasped. "Come inside and sit down and I'll make you
some coffee. When did you last eat?"
Jenny thought for a moment then said, "They gave me a
bowl of porridge at the police station yesterday lunch
time."
He gave her another searching look but simply held the
door open and, feeling like a robot, she walked into the
house and sank into an armchair. She was vaguely aware
of Richard calling Isaac and she heard him telling the boys
that Mummy was tired.
As she looked around the room her eyes rested on an
airmail letter on the mantelpiece. It had not been there
when she left and she did not recognise the writing.

"Who's that from?" she said when Richard brought her a mug of coffee.

A glimmer of a smile lit up Richard's white face. "It's from Bill," he said with animation handing Jenny the letter. "It arrived last Friday. read it."

Jenny took a long draught of coffee then started to read.

2, Bridge Street,
London.
S.E.5.
May 11th.
Dear Dick and Jenny,
I'm sorry we haven't written before. We received your card from Mombasa at Christmas. I hope you are all well and enjoying yourselves in Africa. I expect the boys are quite grown up now. Pam called in last week with her husband. They are going to Indonesia. She said you are working very hard. When are you coming home? Things are going well for us now. I went to a rehabilitation centre for three months and I am now working for my old firm. It's a desk job but it is really good to be back with the fellers again. We are looking forward to seeing you all again. And thanks Dick for everything you did when I was in hospital.
Bye for now,
Bill and Sheila

"That's a nice letter," she said mechanically and handed it back. She sensed that he felt let down by her answer but she was too exhausted to think of anything else to say. Deep down she knew that it was an important letter but she had so many other things to sort out before she could start thinking about Bill and Sheila.

Richard stood looking at her for a moment or two. "You look as if you haven't slept for days. Perhaps you should go to bed after you've had something to eat."

Jenny nodded then shook her head. She hadn't come all this way just to crawl between the sheets. She could smell toast cooking in the kitchen and answered in a dull monotone, "I think I'm hungry more than tired. I didn't sleep too badly on the train last night. Although I didn't get much sleep the night before." Her voice trailed off as she remembered her fight to save James and her face became a musk of pain.

"Let me get you some toast. And another cup of coffee," said Richard hurrying into the kitchen.

He came back with a laden tray and sat in the chair opposite Jenny while she helped herself to some toast and honey. She glanced at her watch and then at Richard. It was half past nine. There was something odd but she wasn't able to work out what. Richard was wearing his white coat so that meant he should be on duty.

She was aware of footsteps outside and then there was a knock at the door. Richard got up and Jenny heard the nurse say, "Sister Ningi wants you in casualty."

Richard gave a gasp of irritation and answered sharply, "Isn't Dr. Fatti there?"

"He's seeing out-patients."

"Then he can help Sister. That's what we always did when there was only one doctor. And Dr. Patel is on duty as well today."

"But what shall I tell Sister Ningi?"

"Tell her that my wife is sick and that I'm looking after her at present. I shall come over later. And I am not to be disturbed again."

Jenny looked puzzled. "Is somebody sick?" she asked as Richard sat down again.

"Sick?"

"You told the nurse that you were looking after a sick person."

Richard looked at Jenny long and hard. "No. I just wanted her to go away."

Suddenly there was a shout of childish laughter from outside and then Darren and David burst into the house their faces creased up with mirth.

"We blew a bubble on a lizard's nose!" chuckled Darren.

"I bet he got a surprise!" said David.

Jenny and Richard looked at each other.

"I bet he did," they said together.

Then looked at each other again.

And laughed.

Printed in Great Britain
by Amazon